THE POLLS ARE IN!

"What's this all about?" Bolt questioned the girl sitting on the ground, her hands tied, her legs bound.

"I tried to vote this morning, and this is what they did to me," she explained, while Bolt worked on the knot at her wrists. He couldn't help but notice her full breasts straining against the dark material, the thin waistline.

The girl smiled defiantly as her hands were freed. But she let Bolt continue his rescue as he began to untie the cloth strip at her ankles. "What's your name?" he asked, observing the shapeliness of her legs.

"Lena Russel." She allowed Bolt to help her to her feet. "I was just trying to exercise my legal right to vote."

Bolt's hand brushed against her full firm breast as he picked her up. Her body was soft and pliable, light as a feather. Her scent was feminine, full of lavender and rose hips. The heady fragrance drifted to Bolt's nostrils, caused a pang of desire to stab at his loins.

"Well, Miss Russel," he encouraged, "if I were the man running for office, yours is one vote I wouldn't want to lose!"

MORE EXCITING WESTERNS FROM ZEBRA!

THE GUNN SERIES BY JORY SHERMAN

GUNN #12: THE WIDOW-MAKER   (987, $2.25)
Gunn offers to help the lovely ladies of Luna Creek when
the ruthless Widow-maker gang kills off their husbands.
It's hard work, but the rewards are mounting!

GUNN #13: ARIZONA HARDCASE   (1039, $2.25)
When a crafty outlaw threatens the lives of some lovely
females, Gunn's temper gets mean and hot—and he's got
no choice but to shoot it off!

GUNN #14: THE BUFF RUNNERS   (1093, $2.25)
Gunn runs into two hell-raising sisters caught in the middle
of a buffalo hunter's feud. He hires out his sharpshooting
skills—and doubles their fun!

THE BOLT SERIES BY CORT MARTIN

BOLT #6: TOMBSTONE HONEYPOT   (1009, $2.25)
In Tombstone, Bolt meets up with luscious Honey
Carberry who tricks him into her beehive. But Bolt has a
stinger of his own!

BOLT #7: RAWHIDE WOMAN   (1057, $2.25)
Rawhide Kate's on the lookout for the man who killed her
family. And when Bolt snatches the opportunity to come to
Kate's rescue, she learns how to handle a tricky gun!

BOLT #8: HARD IN THE SADDLE   (1095, $2.25)
When masked men clean him of his cash, Bolt's left in a
tight spot with a luscious lady. He pursues the gang—and
enjoys a long, hard ride on the way!

*Available wherever paperbacks are sold, or order direct from the
Publisher. Send cover price plus 50¢ per copy for mailing and
handling to Zebra Books, 475 Park Avenue South, New York,
N.Y. 10016. DO NOT SEND CASH.*

#9

BOLT

BADMAN'S BORDELLO
BY CORT MARTIN

ZEBRA BOOKS
KENSINGTON PUBLISHING CORP.

ZEBRA BOOKS

are published by

KENSINGTON PUBLISHING CORP.
475 Park Avenue South
New York, N.Y. 10016

CHAPTER ONE

The sleek brown horse struggled up the last few yards of the steep mountain trail. Without the weight of his rider and the heavy saddlebags, the horse could have made the grade with little effort.

Jared Bolt leaned forward in the saddle, patted his spirited horse on its long thick neck.

"Atta boy, Nick, you can make it," Bolt said, his even voice urging the horse along.

Nick responded to his master's words by tossing his head in the air, snorting through wide flared nostrils. Well-toned muscles rippled beneath the thick hide of Nick's shoulders and forelegs as the horse summoned up the extra strength needed to make it up to the crest of the rugged slope.

Turning in the saddle, Bolt glanced back over his shoulder at his friend, who was following at some distance. Tom Penrod's horse was not as agile as Nick and it lagged behind, its spindly legs awkward as it strained to make the grade.

"Come on, Tom, you're draggin' ass," Bolt called back to his friend.

"Yair. Some short cut you picked!" Tom shouted sarcastically. "I should have known better than to go along with your hair-brained idea. Hell, I could have walked to Cheyenne by now."

"Quit your bellyachin'." Bolt grinned. "We've got it made now. It's all downhill from here on and we'll be in Cheyenne in an hour or so, a full day ahead of schedule."

5

"Don't see what difference it makes," Tom grumbled.

"It doesn't." Bolt faced forward again just as his horse reached the top of the grade. Not prepared for the awesome sight of the landscape below, he sucked in his breath, waited for Tom to catch up with him.

"Ain't that a sight for sore eyes?" Bolt said, his eyes scanning the valley below. Off to the right, the aspens stood stark against the blue sky, their bright yellow leaves topping the straight narrow white trunks. Autumn had been late in coming this year. Even though it was the first week in November, the golden aspen leaves clung tight to their branches. The Cache de la Poudre River shimmered along the base of the Rocky Mountains that rose majestically off to their left.

"Almost worth the trip up here," said Tom, glad that they would be riding downhill the rest of the way. His horse blew air through its extended nostrils.

"You can smell winter in the air," Bolt said, drawing his jacket around him. "Won't be long before the snows settle in this pass. We must be a mile up in the air."

"Yair. Almost makes you feel you could fall off the edge of the earth."

As Bolt studied the panorama of the valley floor below them, he sensed that something was askew.

It was just a dot on the distant landscape, but it didn't escape Bolt's keen eyes. A small dark speck that looked like a black ant from this distance. Perhaps it was a burned out tree stump or something that had fallen from a wagon that had passed that way, since it appeared to be in the open spaces that denoted the trail to Cheyenne.

Bolt's eyes squinted to narrow slits as he studied the dark object, trying to figure out what it was. It was moving! Whatever was down on that road was alive!

"What do you suppose that is?" he asked, pointing at the dark object. "A wounded animal?"

"Where?" Tom asked.

"Right down there. See where the trail goes? Out in the open? At the far end of it."

Tom leaned forward in the saddle, clamped his hands to his forehead, shielding his eyes from the sun. He finally spotted the dark object on the road.

"Jeezus! You're eyes are a damned sight better than mine," said Tom.

"It's good, clean living," Bolt laughed.

"Ha! Tell me about it. Hell, how can you tell from here? Probably a dead coyote or rabbit."

"Not dead. If you watch it for a minute, you'll see it's moving in this direction. Real slow. It looks like a man."

Tom cupped his hands against his eyes so they simulated binoculars. In that way, he zeroed his focus in on the dark object below.

"Yep. He's movin' all right. Somebody musta stole his horse. Nobody'd be dumb enough to be on foot that far from town."

"That's what I was thinking. Something funny's going on."

"Now, Bolt, don't go gettin' yourself all involved. It ain't your problem. Maybe the pilgrim just enjoys walking. He poses no threat to us. If he were planning on jumping us, he certainly wouldn't be out in the open like that. A man planning an ambush don't usually make himself so visible."

"I don't plan on getting involved with a stranger, Tom. You know me better than that."

"Oh, I know you, all right. If that stranger was wearing a skirt, you'd sure as hell get involved. Hell, from here you can't tell whether it's a man or a woman."

7

"Come on. Give me more credit than that."

"You get yourself in more damned trouble helping out pretty women than anyone I know. You'd think by now you'd just pay for a piece of ass and be done with it."

"Not with all the free stuff running around." Bolt grinned.

"You pay for it, Bolt. One way or another. Hell, last month you almost lost every dime you had helping Amylou Lovett."

"Oh? And what about the three thousand greenbacks I left in your care?" Bolt smirked. "I finally heard the whole story on that. You lost that money every time you turned around."

"I'm not talking about that." Tom frowned, turning serious. "Someday you're gonna lose more than your money when you play the gallant hero going to the rescue of some poor gal. It's gonna cost you your life when some jealous husband shoves a rifle butt up your ass."

"Yeah, I have had a couple of close calls at that, but don't worry, I've learned to live and let live. I don't know who that stranger is walking down there on the road, but I suspect there's trouble. We happen to be riding that way and likely we'll pass the stranger, but I don't intend on taking on anyone else's problems."

Tom peered down once more at the dark spot on the landscape that appeared to be moving.

"I just hope he isn't female."

"You worry too much, Tom. And if we don't get going, you'll have something else to worry about."

"What's that?"

"Gettin' to Cheyenne before all the good-looking whores are spoken for."

Bolt pulled the reins to the right, touched his knee to Nick's flanks. The horse threw his head back in response, moved out slowly. The incline down the side of the hill was not nearly as steep as the one had been coming up. The trail wound around the side of the mountain in a gentle sloping path. Nick was sure-footed, stepping carefully over rocks and dodging potholes and ruts in the road caused by recent rains washing across the dirt road.

The floor of the valley was only a few hundred feet below the high pass the two riders had just come through. They would still have to drop down to about 5,000 feet before they reached Cheyenne. The way the trail meandered back and forth, it was impossible for Bolt to keep his eyes on the stranger who walked the lonely road. But every time he had the chance, Bolt studied the dark figure that became a little larger with each turn in the road.

It wasn't until he and Tom emerged on the wide open valley floor that Bolt realized that the figure slowly heading their way was wearing a long skirt or dress.

"Well, I'll be dipped," said Bolt. "It *is* a woman. Wonder what she's doing wandering way out here."

"Oh no you don't," cautioned Tom. "Remember your good intentions."

"The road to hell's paved with good intentions." Bolt grinned as he urged his horse into a gentle trot. "Looks like she's got something hanging around her neck."

"Yair," said Tom, spurring his horse to a faster pace to keep up with Bolt. "Looks like a sign. Suppose she's a walking billboard?"

"Let's find out what she's advertising!"

"Maybe they're giving away free board and lodging to anyone brave enough to come through that pass up there," Tom said drily as he glanced back up over his shoulder at the place where he and his friend had been a few minutes earlier.

By the time Bolt was within fifty yards of the darkly

clothed woman, he could tell that she was blindfolded with a strip of dark cloth across her eyes. He couldn't yet read the sign that hung from her neck.

When he rode up to within twenty yards of the staggering woman, he noticed that her hands were behind her back, probably tied together. He glanced down at her feet to see if her ankles were tied together, but could not see them because of the long dress. The funny way she was walking, with short shuffling steps, made him think they were bound together.

He squinted his eyes, tried to read the sign.

Suddenly, the woman, frightened by the sound of approaching hoofbeats, turned sideways, tried to scuffle away from the road.

"Wait, ma'am!" Bolt called. "Don't try to run!"

"No! No!" screamed the woman hysterically when she heard Bolt's voice. "Leave me alone! Don't hit me anymore!" She tried to scramble away, but could only take short steps. In her attempt to get away from the approaching strangers, she tripped over her own feet which were tied together at the ankles with strips of cloth.

She stumbled and fell to the hard ground head first, unable to break her fall because her hands were also tied together, behind her back. The cardboard sign around her neck ground into the dirt beneath her. The dark brown hat she was wearing tumbled off her head, scooted across the ground.

Bolt rode up quickly, slid down from his saddle. He walked over to her, leaned down.

"Let me help you, ma'am," he said, his voice gentle.

"No!" she screamed. "Get away from me!" She kicked out blindly, both feet aiming for the masculine voice she heard near her.

Bolt jumped back, dodged the feet that kicked like a mule.

"Settle down, miss!" Bolt ordered. "I'll untie you if you'll give me half a chance."

"Don't you touch me, you beast!" she screamed, her voice shrill and hostile. She kicked out again and again, scooting away from the strange voice. She rolled over on her back, kicked out with even more power.

Bolt tried to reach her arms, side-stepped her vicious kicks.

Tom grinned as he rode up alongside the struggling couple.

"Looks like you got a spirited filly on your hands."

"You could give me a hand, Tom, instead of sitting up there with that shit-eating grin on your face."

"Thought you weren't going to get involved with other people's troubles," Tom said mockingly.

"I ain't," Bolt said, glaring at Tom, "but you can't just ride on and leave the poor woman bound and blindfolded. She'd likely die before morning."

Tom threw his leg across the saddle and dismounted.

The woman kicked again.

"Go away! Both of you! Don't hurt me!"

"Don't look like she wants our help," Tom said, backing away.

Bolt moved around behind the squirming woman, reached for her shoulder. When he touched her, she let out an ear-piercing scream.

"Jeezus, woman!" Bolt said, "we're just trying to help you. We mean you no harm."

He grabbed both shoulders firmly, held her while Tom came close enough to untie the blindfold that was knotted at the back of her head. Bolt released his hold on her when the blindfold had been thrown to the ground.

The woman, now in a sitting position, cowered away from the two strange men, turning her head to look at them.

11

"Please don't hurt me," she said, her voice soft and pleading. "Do you . . . you work for . . . Jack Sanders?"

"Who in the hell is Jack Sanders?" Tom asked.

"Is he the man who did this to you?" Bolt said. He saw the fear in her bright blue eyes. He was surprised that underneath the smudges of dirt on her face, she was quite beautiful. And much younger than he had first thought when he had seen her dark brown dress.

"Y . . . yes," she stuttered. "He hit me. He hurt me. Oh, please don't hurt me anymore."

"We won't." Bolt walked around in front of her as Tom began unfastening the knot of the cloth binding her wrists together behind her. Bolt reached for the thick paper sign that hung around her neck, pulled it up over her long dark hair and stared at it. Painted in crude lettering was the message: I TRIED TO VOTE AND THIS IS WHAT I GOT.

"What's this all about?" he said.

The girl brought her freed hands around in front of her, rubbed the raw wrists. She sat on the ground, her bound legs straight out in front of her.

Bolt leaned down and began to untie the cloth strip at her ankles. He couldn't help but notice her full breasts straining against the dark material, the thin waistline. She had a sharp patrician nose that was smudged with dirt, full sensual lips and blue eyes that were as innocent as a child's.

"Just what the sign says," she said, heaving a sigh. "I tried to vote this morning and this is what they did to me. I just turned twenty-one last week and I was looking forward to voting for the first time. But they wouldn't let me."

"What's your name?" Bolt asked, noticing her trim ankles as he removed the strip of cloth and threw it to the ground.

"Lena Russel." She allowed Bolt to help her to her feet. "I was just trying to exercise my legal right to vote."

Bolt's hand brushed against her full firm breast as he picked her up. Her body was soft and pliable, light as a feather. Her scent was feminine, full of lavender and rose hips. The heady fragrance drifted to Bolt's nostrils, caused a pang of desire to stab at his loins.

He cleared the husk from his voice before he spoke.

"I heard the women were voting in Wyoming now. Lena, why would this Sanders feller stop you from voting?"

"I don't really know. The Wyoming legislature passed women's suffrage back in 1869, nine years ago. It was the first state to do so. Passing that act was supposed to attract single women of marriageable age into the state. I can remember how my father felt about the passing of that act."

"Was he for it or against it?" Tom asked.

"Oh, he was completely for it. You see, my mother died when I was very young and my father always wanted to remarry so that I'd have another mother to raise me. Papa used to take me to all the town gatherings when Anna Dickinson crusaded for the passage of women's suffrage back in '69. I think it was because of her promise of luring young women to Cheyenne that the men voted for it. But it didn't work out that way. Papa never did get married again."

"Is he still alive?"

"No, he died a couple of years ago. But one of our friends, Louisa Ann Swain, was the first woman to vote. She was seventy years old and I remember Papa took me to the polls that day to watch her enter the voting booth. It was quite an event and the whole town turned out to witness it. Back then, the men wanted women to vote because they thought a lot of women

13

would come here. I was only twelve at the time, but ever since then I've dreamed of the time when I could cast my own ballot. And then this happens." She clutched at her breasts, glared over at the ugly cardboard sign that was now on the ground.

"Were you the only woman who tried to vote this morning?" Bolt asked.

"No. I went to the polls with a group of women, but none of us were allowed to vote. The other girls backed off when they were threatened. I was the only one who stuck to my guns. Jack Sanders and a couple of his men brought me out here and turned me loose after they tied me up and blindfolded me."

Bolt stared into Lena's innocent blue eyes.

"You want to go back to Cheyenne and vote? You still have time."

"Oh, mercy sakes," she said, "I wouldn't dare try it again. It's not just me I'm thinking about. You see, I own a small bordello in Cheyenne and some of my girls, the ones who were old enough to go to the polls with me, were mistreated for trying to vote. I saw the looks in the eyes of the men who chased them back to the bordello. I heard their lewd remarks. Sanders' men, every last one of them."

"Ain't that a coincidence," Tom Penrod laughed. "Bolt is the owner of several bordellos and we're heading to Cheyenne to look the place over, see about opening another one there."

"You own some . . . whorehouses . . . ?" Lena said, looking at Bolt as if she was seeing him for the first time.

"Yep." Bolt smiled. "Anything wrong with that?"

"No . . . I mean . . . you just don't look like the type."

"Neither do you," Bolt laughed. "Now, you want to go back and vote? Tom and I will accompany you to

14

the polls and see that you're allowed to exercise your rights."

She thought about it for a minute.

"No, I don't dare go back there. When Jack Sanders left me off out here, he said he was taking over the Lilac House. That's my bordello. I feel sorry for my girls with Jack being in charge, but he warned me that those girls would suffer a worse fate if I returned. I couldn't live with myself if they were hurt because of me."

"They're suffering anyway if Sanders is anything like you say."

"He's far worse than I can describe," Lena sighed.

"Then we're taking you back," Bolt said flatly. "And you're going to vote."

"No!" Lena reached out a hand and grabbed Bolt's arm. "Sanders will kill you if he sees you with me!"

"He might," Bolt said as he led Lena to his horse, lifted her up in his saddle. He glanced back at Tom, saw the dirty look in Tom's eyes.

"Bolt, you promised . . ." Tom said.

"What did you promise, Mister Bolt?" Lena asked.

Grinning at Tom, Bolt climbed up in the saddle, settled himself in front of the young woman.

"What Tom's trying to say is that we're always glad to help out a lovely lady in distress."

CHAPTER TWO

As the trio rode into Cheyenne, Bolt didn't have to ask Lena Russel where the polling place was. The minute they entered the main street of the town, he saw the crowd of men milling around the street, the line that formed on the boardwalk in front of one of the falsefronts.

Lena tightened her grip around Bolt's waist, leaned forward in the saddle to say something in his ear.

"Bolt, I don't think we should go through with this. Look at all those men!"

"They're just voters," Bolt said as he turned his head. "With no more rights than you."

"But they'll cause trouble again if I show up."

"Not with Tom and me there to see that you're protected. You can do it."

Lena took a deep breath, held it as if to build her courage. She leaned into Bolt's back, her ample breasts pushing into him. Her hands squeezed even harder around his waist.

"Let's go for it," she said.

Bolt felt the pressure of her breasts on his back, the warmth of her loins at his buttocks. Her feminine scent surrounded him as she leaned into him. He liked her spunk, hoped that she would remain determined enough to actually cast a vote. He rode on, headed for the crowd of men that loitered around the polling place some two blocks ahead.

Deliberately keeping Nick's pace slow, Bolt kept to the opposite side of the street from where the men gathered to vote and discuss the politics of the day. Only a few of the men bothered to look their way as they stopped across the street from the Town Hall. Bolt pulled back on Nick's reins, noticed that the crowd appeared to be orderly, although a bit boisterous. He dismounted, helped Lena down from the saddle. Tom rode up behind him, dismounted. Tom and Bolt walked the horses a few feet to the hitching post in front of the Eddy Street Saloon, which was located directly across the street from the Town Hall where the voting was in progress.

As they were looping the reins around the hitch rail, Bolt turned to Lena, spoke to her in a loud whisper.

"Do you see Jack Sanders over there?"

Lena stood close to Bolt, turned around slowly to study the faces in the crowd. Her stomach quivered with fear as she remembered her previous visit to the polling place early that morning. Pain surged through her bruised body as she recalled how Sanders had slapped her around, kicked at her legs, humiliated her in general before he snatched her away to blindfold and bind her and dump her on the deserted road that led away from Cheyenne.

"No, I don't see Sanders," she whispered. "But one of the men who works for him is over there."

"Who's that?" Bolt said without turning around to look across the street.

"Curtis Dillman. He's up on the porch, near the voting booth. Leaning against the wall. I don't think he noticed us. At least he's not looking this way. Or maybe he saw us and doesn't care."

Bolt glanced up, saw the colorful banners that adorned the windows of the saloon. Red, white and blue streamers hung down from the banners that boasted praise for one candidate or another. Other patriotic streamers were draped around the doorway of the saloon. Handbills and small cards proclaiming the virtues of various politicians littered the boardwalk and the street. A hand-lettered sign in the window of the saloon announced: The Eddy Street Saloon is the only place to celebrate. Come in for a drink after you vote! Drinks half price for voters! Free for the winners!

Cheyenne, like other towns in the west, would be full of loud and unruly drunks that election night. After the polls were closed, men would migrate to the saloons to wait for the counting of the ballots to be completed, to celebrate. Men tended to use the elections as an excuse to get riproaring drunk and Bolt guessed that was as good an excuse as any other.

Turning away from the saloon, he faced the crowd that had gathered across the street. A couple of wagons parked near the town hall displayed campaign banners for different candidates. Some of the men at the edge of the street wore arm bands fashioned from red, white and blue ribbons. Others showed their patriotism by wearing the colors around their hat brims. Some wore campaign buttons with catchy slogans on bright blue or red shirts. An air of anticipation rippled through the crowd as the men watched the voting action. It was as if the onlookers believed that just being witness to the event could influence the way the votes were cast. The line of prospective voters who waited their turn on the boardwalk below the porch had dwindled to three men, but others would be along until the polls closed.

Still standing beside the hitchrail in front of the Eddy Street Saloon, Bolt watched the crowd, his eyes scanning the faces, then moving up to the porch where the curtained voting booth was positioned near the doorway of the town hall.

Bolt saw the man Lena had mentioned. Curtis Dillman. The tall, lanky man was still leaning against the wall, between the voting booth and the doorway of the building. He was looking toward the dark blue curtains of the booth, his hat brim pulled down low so it covered his eyes. A six-shooter was tied low around his leg. Bolt didn't think Dillman had spotted them, but it would be impossible for Lena to vote without drawing his attention.

On the other side of the doorway, three well-dressed men sat around a long table. Two of the men sat behind the table, their backs to the wall. The third man sat on a chair at the far end of the table, facing the doorway and the voting booth. Sitting on the table in front of him were two wooden crates that served as the ballot boxes.

The dark curtains of the voting booth parted and a man stepped out, a long printed sheet of paper clutched in his hand. A spontaneous cheer went up from the crowd as the man emerged from the cramped booth, even though the onlookers had no way of knowing how the man had voted. The voter carried the ballot over to the long table, where the man guarding the ballot boxes nodded to him. The voter folded the ballot, then shoved it into one of the ballot boxes, turned and walked down the steps.

Several men gathered around the voter as he stepped down into their midst, asked questions about how he had voted. The man grinned, but would not divulge his choices of candidates.

Like clockwork, the next man in line stepped forward, walked up the steps, moved over to stand before the long table. After a brief exchange of words, the new voter, a tall elderly gentleman, was given a ballot. He carried the printed sheet over to the voting booth, disappeared behind the curtains. Only his legs, from his knees to his shoes, were visible below the curtain.

"We'll wait for the others to vote before we take you over there," Bolt said to Lena. "Less chance for trouble that way."

"I hope you're right," she said, stepping close to him. "There's not another woman in sight."

Bolt felt the warmth of her body, the slight tremble of her hand as she touched his arm. He looked down at her and smiled.

"Looks like you're the only one brave enough to stand up and be counted. Just remember, your vote is just as important as any man's." He squeezed her hand, then turned back to watch the election process. He ran his hand across the butt of his holstered pistol, glanced at Tom. Tom nodded, patted his own pistol to let Bolt know he was ready.

It seemed like it took the remaining voters a long time to mark their ballots and push them into the ballot boxes. Finally, when the last man in line climbed the steps and stood before the table to get his ballot, Bolt was ready to make his move.

He stepped over to his horse, removed the sign that Lena had worn around her neck from the saddle horn, the sign that said, "I TRIED TO VOTE AND THIS IS WHAT I GOT." Tucking it under his arm so the lettering didn't show, he looked at Lena.

"You ready to vote?"

"Yes. I guess so."

"Tom, I'm going to escort Lena to the voting booth. I want you to stand down on the boardwalk by the porch over there and keep your eyes peeled for trouble."

Tom nodded.

Bolt led the way across the street, Lena walking between him and Tom. They reached the crowd of men just as the last voter emerged from the voting booth. The usual cheer went up from the men as the voter walked over to the table to deposit his ballot in a wooden crate.

"Pardon me," Bolt said to one of the men at the back

edge of the crowd. The heavy set man turned around, gasped when he saw Lena with Bolt and Tom. He stepped aside quickly to let the trio by him. As Bolt threaded his way through the crowd, the men parted to make room for him to make it up to the steps. A shocked silence fell over the gathering as the men realized what was happening. Bolt felt the tension in the air. It was different from the note of anticipation that had been there a minute before. It was a hushed atmosphere with men sensing trouble. All heads turned in Bolt's direction as he and Lena approached the steps. No one spoke.

As the wave of silence washed across the crowd and reached the porch, Curt Dillman pushed himself away from the wall, stood tall and looked down at the crowd to see what had caused the sudden stillness. His eyes fell on Lena Russel who was at the foot of the stairs. He glared at her, started to speak when he saw the two men who flanked her. He noticed that both of the strangers were armed with holstered pistols.

Bolt returned his stare, allowed Dillman to look him over before he moved. Dillman was tall and muscular, probably a couple of inches taller than six feet, Bolt figured. His dark, shaggy hair extended beyond the grimy hat, the dirty, matted strands clinging to Dillman's neck. His feral eyes were wild and mean, muddy brown.

Dillman stepped forward, to the edge of the porch, where he took up a stance with feet spread apart, as if to block Lena's passage. He jammed his hands on his hips in a threatening gesture. His hand was within easy reach of his hog-tied pistol.

Bolt moved on up to the first step, looked back at Lena who took a tentative step up to join him. Tom took one long stride away from the wooden-plank steps, positioned himself in front of the porch, almost directly below the voting booth. From there he could watch what happened on the porch as well as keep an eye on the crowd of men who were surging forward to get a better view of the woman and the strangers.

The boards creaked as Bolt stepped up to the second stair. The crowd was perfectly still except for a nervous cough, the hushed shuffle of feet and they elbowed closer.

Lena moved up to the second step, stood beside Bolt.

"You ain't comin' up here to vote, Miss Russel," Dillman said, his voice loud and threatening.

"You a member of the Election Committee, Mr. Dillman?" Bolt asked.

"Don't need to be to keep her from voting," Dillman snarled. "She already knows that."

"You mean this sign?" Bolt took the cardboard placard from under his arm, held it up in the air.

The crowd of men began to call out loud remarks.

"Hang the sign around her neck!" shouted one ruffian near the back.

"No women allowed to vote in Cheyenne!" yelled another riled onlooker.

"Let her vote!" called an elderly man near the steps. His voice was drowned out by the angry cries of others who were opposed to Lena's voting.

"No! We don't want no harlots voting here!"

"Down with women voters!"

The chant was picked up by the agitated mob. "Down with women voters! Down with women voters!"

Bolt knew that the sentiments of the crowd were with Dillman and not with Lena Russel. It could get sticky before Lena got to the voting booth.

As Bolt moved up one more step, Dillman's hand floated from his waist, down his leg, until it was just above the butt of his pistol. The hand hung there, a silent threat if Bolt took another step. Bolt moved his own hand slowly, let it hover above his own holster.

"She's not voting here!" Dillman challenged.

"You may have to back up those words with action," Bolt said as he saw a man move to the front of the crowd and take up a position in front of the porch. Bolt glanced over at the man, saw that he wore the tin badge of a sheriff.

The lawman stood with his arms folded across his chest. He watched the shouting men with darting eyes, but made no move to disperse the mob.

Bolt noticed Dillman glance over at the sheriff. Dillman's hand automatically retreated to his waistline, but the tall man stood steadfast at the head of the stairs, glaring down at Bolt.

Bolt pressed his advantage, moved up the remaining two steps, pulling Lena with him. He stepped around Dillman, took Lena over to the long table where the ballots were stacked and ready for the voters. Bolt looked at each of the three men seated at the table. They stared back, not moving.

"You three men on the Election Committee?" Bolt said, his eyes sweeping across the three faces.

"Yes," said the closest man, his eyes noncommittal. He wore a neatly crimped hat, a clean shirt, suspenders, plain gray arm bands to keep his long sleeves from dragging across the papers and pencils on the table in front of him.

"What's your name?" Bolt asked.

"I'm Lester Townsend. This is Joel Adams and the man at the end of the table is Mister Parker Franklin."

"I assume you men are here to see that the rules of the election are observed and carried out."

The three men nodded dumbly.

"Is this a fair election, Mr. Franklin?" Bolt said, swinging around to face the man at the end.

"Oh, yes, sir. Only eligible voters are allowed to vote and I'm in charge of the ballot box." Franklin patted the wooden crate in front of him that bore the legend: *Telegraph Matches* on the side. The wood was sturdy and the old match box had been converted to a ballot box by notching a slot in the heavy lid.

"And is this a legal election? Are all of the rules being followed, executed?" Bolt's eyes locked on Franklin's for a moment, then shifted to the other two men.

"It's an honest election, if that's what you're gettin' at," said Joel Adams. His hand rested on the stack of fresh, unmarked ballots in front of him.

"Are women legally allowed to vote in Cheyenne?" Bolt asked.

"Yes," said Adams, shifting uneasily in his chair.

"Do you know Miss Lena Russel to be an eligible voter? Of legal age?" Bolt persisted in his questioning, making his point clear to all the witnesses.

"Yes," said Lester Townsend, sticking his thumbs behind his suspenders. "We proclaimed her to be a legal voter when she was here today, early this morning. I reckon her status hasn't changed."

"Then none of you men on the Election Committee has any objection if she exercises her legal right to vote now?" Bolt's voice boomed as he let the question hang in the air.

"No," said Townsend in a low voice as he glanced back at Curt Dillman.

Dillman glared at the three men seated at the table, then glanced at the sheriff down below. The sheriff seemed to be enjoying the confrontation and made no move to stop Miss Russel from voting or to see that she was allowed to vote without endangering herself.

As Townsend handed Lena her ballot, the throng of men began to boo and chant again. "Down with women voters! Down with women voters!"

Lena took the ballot. Bolt led her across the porch to the voting booth, walking in front of Dillman who glared at him with muddy brown eyes.

Lena stepped inside the voting booth, her ballot clutched in her hand. She pulled the curtain closed behind her. Only the long skirt of her dark brown dress showed beneath the curtain.

Bolt took up a post just outside the voting booth, his hand within easy reach of his pistol. He glanced down at Tom. Tom smiled, then turned his attention back to the crowd of men who were hooting and hollering while Lena was voting. Bolt watched Curt Dillman carefully, expected the grubby man to make a move.

The time ticked by as the onlookers became more agitated, more boisterous. It was obvious to Bolt that most of the men assembled before the polling place disapproved of women voters. Bolt glanced at the blue curtains of the booth, wished Lena would hurry and get her voting done so they could leave before the crowd became unruly. Seconds ticked by. They seemed like hours.

Finally, he heard the rustle of her skirt, the shuffle of her shoes as she turned around in the booth, preparing to exit. She drew the curtain aside, stood there for a brief instant with her neatly folded ballot in her hands, then took Bolt's arm.

"We did it," she whispered as he escorted her back across the porch to the ballot box which Parker Franklin was guarding.

Not yet, Bolt wanted to tell her. Her vote didn't count until it was officially placed inside the wooden crate at the far end of the table.

Curt Dillman mumbled something as they passed in front of him, but Bolt couldn't make out the words.

Bolt deposited Lena Russel in front of Mr. Franklin and the ballot box. Mr. Franklin nodded to the wooden crate, indicating that she should put the ballot into the notched slot on the top of the box.

She leaned forward, proudly placed the folded ballot into the slot. Jamming against the other ballots already inside the box, Lena's ballot stuck out of the slot. She leaned over farther, tapped it to force it on inside.

Just as she leaned over, a shot rang out from the back of the crowd.

The ballot slid on into the box as Bolt reacted to the boom of the shot. He pushed her aside, heard the bullet whiz by his head, where her shoulder had been an instant before. He grabbed her arm, pulled her away from the table as a second shot rang out in the air. The shot came from the same direction, from the back of the crowd.

The sheriff snapped into action, dashed toward the back of the crowd to find the gunman. Confusion ran through the mob as some men ducked instinctively when they heard the gunshots, while others began to scatter.

Tom Penrod watched the crowd carefully, but also kept his eyes on the porch, where Bolt and Lena were.

Bolt led Lena away from the table after the second shot cracked the air. The three election workers scooted their chairs back, ducked under the table for protection from the gunfire.

Bolt and Lena darted to the middle of the porch where they once again passed in front of Curt Dillman. They turned to run down the stairs.

Before Bolt could take the first step down the wooden stairs, he knew he misjudged the situation. He had thought it would be easy to slip away with Lena Russel in the confusion that followed the shooting. He hadn't counted on Dillman making a move at this stage of the game, especially since Lena had already voted.

Bolt felt the hard cold metal shoved against the back

of his head. The cold barrel of Dillman's pistol.

A second later he felt Dillman's hot breath on the back of his neck as the man leaned close.

"You shouldn't have pushed the issue," Dillman said, his foul breath assaulting Bolt's nostrils. "You won't live long enough to take another step. Neither will Miss Russel."

A cold chill ran up Bolt's spine, raised the hackles on the back of his neck. He felt the pistol barrel jam against his head, heard the ominous click of the gun being cocked. He couldn't even turn around to face his killer.

His eyes fell on the men below him. They were all scattering in different directions. None of them looked up to the porch to see what was happening.

None of them cared.

CHAPTER THREE

Bolt stood frozen in his tracks for just an instant. That's all the time he had to think. With the sheriff distracted and out of sight, Curt Dillman had suddenly become brave. If Bolt made the wrong move now, his brains would be splattered all over the steps, the porch.

With one swift, smooth motion, Bolt shoved Lena Russel aside, drew his elbow straight back with a hard jab to Dillman's stomach.

A loud ooooomph emitted from Dillman's mouth as the blow knocked the wind out of him.

Before the surprised Dillman could pull the trigger, Bolt whirled around, knocked the heavy pistol from the gunman's hand. It clattered to the porch with a jarring crash. The sudden jolt caused the pistol to go off. A roaring blast rocked the air.

Someone screamed from behind them. Not a woman's scream, but a heavy scream from one of the men on the porch. A chair toppled over, crashed on the wooden surface of the porch. The man who had been hit by the unaimed shot moaned in pain, fell to the floor with a thud.

Bolt didn't have time to look around to see who had taken the wild bullet. Dillman lunged at him like a crazy man, both hands swinging, his brown eyes wild with hatred.

Bolt ducked the hammering fists, let go with a hard blow to Dillman's gut.

Dillman tightened up his stomach muscles so that Bolt's fist bounced off the taut flesh. The tall, muscular man straightened his hand to a stiff knife, crashed it down on the side of Bolt's neck, right at the collarbone.

The fierce blow caught the muscled cord in Bolt's neck. Blinding pain shot through to his brain. Splotches of bright colors blossomed inside his head as his mind fogged over in a haze. He struggled to stay alert. His knees became rubbery and he fought to remain upright. He glanced up just in time to see the tall, mean-eyed man draw his fist back to make another swing.

With pain searing through his neck and shoulder, Bolt managed to duck away from the powerful blow.

Dillman's fist plowed into thin air. He cursed as his thrust threw him forward.

Bolt saw that he had a brief advantage. He brought a swift, staggering uppercut into the crude man's jaw.

Dillman's head snapped back from the force of the blow. He groaned as his neck cracked. His dirty, wrinkled hat flew off his head, sailed to the ground. His thick arms flailed the air as he tried to strike out at Bolt's face. He missed his target as Bolt dodged the powerful fists.

Bolt got in a quick jab to Dillman's cheek with his left hand, then drove his right fist into the other side of Dillman's face. He felt the flesh give under his blow as Dillman's face contorted grotesquely.

Blood spurted from Dillman's nose, trickled down across his lips, chin, spattered onto his shirt. The angry man wiped a finger under his nose, saw the blood where it dripped on his hand. His beady eyes filled with a new hatred, an uncontrollable anger. His hands darted out toward Bolt. He grabbed Bolt by the shoulders and threw him back against the porch railing.

The crowd of men gathered below the porch started hollering at the first sight of blood, at the roughness of the fight. Caught up in the excitement of the scuffle,

29

they clamored for more bloodshed, shouted for harder punches, deadly blows. They didn't seem to care who won the fight as long as it was rough and dirty.

Bolt felt his back slam into the hard wooden porch rail. For an instant, it felt like his spine had snapped in two, like his ribs had cracked and were puncturing something inside him. He tried to straighten up, found that he couldn't move because of the burning pain. He thought he was paralyzed.

Dillman was on him again, instantly, before Bolt could find the right muscles to move out of the strong man's way. Suddenly, Dillman's thick, powerful hands were wrapped around Bolt's neck. Dillman pushed Bolt with such force that Bolt was bent over backwards, draped over the porch rail. The huge hands began to tighten around Bolt's throat, squeezing his air passage closed.

"You got no business here, stranger," Dillman growled as his fingers tightened around Bolt's neck. "We don't take to no pissant drifters stickin' their snotty noses in where they don't belong. You shoulda left the girl alone. She spells trouble in this town."

Bolt gasped for breath. His mouth hung open but he couldn't draw any air into his lungs. He felt his eyes begin to bulge as the blood flow was cut off. His brain started to go blank as the strong fingers seemed to be squeezing the life from him. He brought his hands up, tried to push the big man away from him, but he had no strength in his arms. He couldn't find the leverage he needed to shove the man away. He sensed the tension mounting in the crowd below, felt their eyes on him. He wondered where his friend, Tom Penrod, was. He wondered how he could get out of his situation.

The fingers squeezed harder. Bolt tried to squirm away from Dillman's clutches, but he had little strength left. He thought about the expression he'd heard that said your whole life flashed in front of you when you were dying. Well, it just wasn't true. You fought for your life right up to the very last moment. He tried to move again, but the fingers just got tighter around his throat. His mind dulled, fogged over with a dark haze. He felt like there was just one thread left to his brain, just enough to keep him from losing consciousness. He forced himself to think. He had to get free of the brute who was trying to kill him.

Concentrating all his efforts, Bolt finally made his move. With all the strength he could muster, he brought his right knee up, slammed it into Dillman's groin. Instantly, he felt the fingers loosen from his throat. He gasped, drew in a quick breath.

Curt Dillman's hands flew to his crotch. He doubled over, cursed the pain that shot through his loins like an arrow.

Bolt gulped in another breath, came up fighting. The crushing pain in his back had numbed to a dull ache. He smashed a fist into Dillman's face, plowed his face again before Dillman could bring his fists up to defend himself. Bolt connected with two blows to Dillman's temples, staggering the big man.

Dillman's body began to sway as he careened backwards. He slammed into the wall of the building. His arms flew out as he struggled to keep his balance. One arm struck the voting booth, sent it crashing to the ground.

Bolt was on him before the big man could regain his balance. He battered Dillman's face with one blow after the other. Each blow sent the back of Dillman's head crashing against the hard wood of the building. Bolt didn't let up on his attack, even when Dillman's legs became wobbly, even when the big man's eyes glazed over with the empty stare of an idiot.

His brain numbed from the fierce punches, Dillman's mouth fell open as he took still another one of Bolt's punishing blows to the head. It took all of his concentration and effort just to double up his fist, draw his arm back. His jab at Bolt's head was in slow motion. He had lost all the power behind the punch. His limp fist brushed against Bolt's chin like it was a powder puff. He tried to strike out at Bolt again, but his muscles wouldn't respond to the commands of his jumbled brains. He shook his head, tried to clear the cobwebs from his mind. He drew his fist back again.

Bolt smashed into Dillman's temple with a driving fist, leashing out with all his strength.

Dillman's head snapped back. Further dazed from the blow, he reeled back against the wall with the full weight of his body. Flooded with renewed anger, he jabbed out with useless fists. Unable to focus on the enemy, his hands pawed the air. He was like a punch-drunk fighter, trained to keep punching until the bell sounded.

The crowd called out, demanding more action.

Bolt took two quick steps backwards, drew his leg up, then smashed the heel of his boot straight into Dillman's groin.

Dillman screamed out in pain, but his scream was lost in the cheers that thundered out from the onlookers. Caught up in the action, they loved the fight.

Curt Dillman clutched at his crotch as his body slid down the wall and oozed to the floor of the porch. Groaning in pain, he rolled on the floor, rocked back and forth with his hands between his legs.

The shouts from the frenzied crowd became louder as they called for more action.

Fearing that some of the men would come after him, Bolt glanced around quickly. None of them headed for the porch. They were busy slapping each other on the back, hooting and discussing the outcome of the fight.

Bolt's eyes came back to the porch, searched for Lena. He spotted her over by the table. She was stooped down, tending to Lester Townsend. The man's shoe and sock had been removed and from what Bolt could see, the wound from the wild bullet was only superficial. A slight crease where the bullet had grazed the back of his leg. Joel Adams and Parker Franklin, his fellow election workers, watched as Lena dabbed at the bleeding wound with a clean handkerchief. She looked at Bolt when she felt his eyes on her. He saw the fear in her blue eyes, her pale face that had drained of color.

Bolt brought his attention back to Dillman as the downed man tried to scoot across the floor toward the doorway of the building. Bolt looked down, saw Dillman's pistol near the door. Taking two quick steps, he ground his boot heel into Dillman's hand just as Dillman reached for the weapon.

Dillman screamed again.

The men in the crowd pressed forward, craned their necks to see what they were missing.

Bolt leaned over, picked up Dillman's pistol.

"This what you're after?" he said, holding the pistol up in the air.

Dillman glared at him.

Bolt wiped the dust from the barrel of the pistol, shoved it into his waistband.

It was then that he noticed someone else on the porch. As he glanced beyond the toppled voting booth, he saw his friend Penrod standing at the far end. Bolt hadn't noticed Tom come up on the porch, but he was there, leaning against the railing, his arms folded across his chest.

Tom grinned at Bolt. He tipped his hat back on his head, gave Bolt a nod of approval.

Bolt swore an oath under his breath. He wanted to wipe that silly grin off his friend's face. Curt Dillman had nearly choked him to death and Tom hadn't come to his aid.

Bolt spotted the sign that Lena had worn around her neck. It was on the floor near Tom, where it had fallen during the scuffle. He hated the injustice of the whole thing. Men had voted the suffrage law into effect and yet Lena Russel had been humiliated just because she tried to exercise her right to vote. She had been forced to wear that sign and then she had been dumped outside of town, bound and blindfolded, to wander around lost and frightened. All because a man named Jack Sanders hadn't wanted Lena to vote. There was more to it than the voting issue, Bolt knew. Sanders had wanted to take over Lena's bordello, the Lilac House. Well, it wasn't fair and Curtis Dillman was a part of it. He was a friend of Sanders.

"Tom, hand me that sign, will you?"

Tom walked over to the cardboard sign, picked it up and carried it to Bolt.

"Get up, Dillman," Bolt ordered. "You're gonna eat some humble pie."

Dillman gave Bolt a dirty look, then slowly pulled himself up. He leaned against the wall defiantly.

"Over here," Bolt gestured. "I want to make sure everyone can see you."

Dillman hesitated, looked at Bolt's holstered pistol, then at his own pistol tucked in Bolt's waistband. He slowly walked to the porch railing near the steps where Bolt was standing.

Bolt started to hang the sign around Dillman's neck, but he had a better idea. Eat humble pie, he thought. That's just what Dillman was going to do. He held the cardboard sign with one hand, tore a small piece of it from one end.

"Open your mouth," Bolt said.

"But . . . but I . . ." Dillman said.

Bolt stuffed a chunk of the sign into Dillman's mouth when he started to protest.

The men watching laughed.

Dillman spit the chunk of cardboard out.

Bolt tore off another piece.

"You're gonna eat this," Bolt said. He crammed the second piece of cardboard inside Dillman's mouth. "Chew on that for a while!"

Again, the crowd laughed.

Dillman opened his mouth, started to spit the damp cardboard out.

"I said eat it," Bolt said. "Swallow it."

Dillman choked and gagged, finally swallowed the small piece.

Bolt shredded the sign into small particles, stuffed them into Dillman's mouth until he was satisfied that Dillman was sick enough to remember the incident for a long time to come.

"I won't forget this," Dillman said, his voice full of hatred.

"That's the whole idea," Bolt told him. "And you can tell your boss, Jack Sanders, to expect a visit from us."

"You won't last five minutes against Sanders," Dillman snarled. "You just got lucky with me, but I wouldn't push your luck. If I were you, I'd get out of town while the gettin's still good. And I'd take that little tramp with you."

Bolt ignored Dillman's threats.

"If you want your pistol back," Bolt said, "you can pick it up at the sheriff's office. I'll tell him to take good care of it for you."

"You sonofabitch," Dillman mumbled. "You'll be sorry you ever laid eyes on me."

"I already am." Bolt turned and walked over to

Lena. He took her arm and led her down the stairs.

Tom followed them as Bolt walked around the group of men and headed across the street where their horses were tied to the hitchrail in front of the Eddy Street Saloon. When they were well away from the others, Bolt turned to Tom.

"Where in the hell were you when I needed you?"

"Right there, watching the whole thing. You didn't think I'd miss you in action, did you?"

"Jeezus. Dillman nearly choked me to death and you just stood there with your thumb up your ass."

"I knew you could do it, Bolt." Tom grinned. "Besides, wouldn't have been a fair fight if I'd come to your rescue and I know how much you believe in a fair fight."

"Shit! Men like that don't know how to be fair."

"Well the crowd wouldn't have enjoyed it nearly as much if it had been two against one. You gave 'em their money's worth. Hell, I even enjoyed it."

"Thanks, Tom. I'll remember that next time you need a little help. But right now you're gonna buy us some supper. My belly button's rubbing against my back bone. You know a good place to eat, Lena?"

"There are several good places in town," she said. "The Cheyenne Hotel has a nice restaurant and the hotel is a good place to stay."

"Expensive, I hope. Tom's buyin'."

"Expensive enough, but the food's good."

"Good. Tom, take this gun to the sheriff's office and meet us at the Cheyenne Hotel."

Tom took Dillman's pistol from Bolt, tucked it into his waistband while he untied his horse. He grinned at Bolt, then turned and rode off.

"Is there a livery stable around here?" Bolt asked Lena. "I think I'll put Nick up for the night. I have no intention of being out among the election celebrations tonight. I think it's a good time to tuck yourself in and stay inside."

"A good time indeed to stay in bed," Lena said.

Bolt wondered how she meant it. There was a husk to her voice that hadn't been there before. There was also a twinkle to her bright blue eyes, a tilt to her smile. Damned if it didn't sound like an invitation.

"There's a livery around the corner and down the street," she said. "I'll show you."

Facing the banner-covered saloon, Bolt began to untie Nick's reins. Lena stood in front of him, off to his left. He felt her eyes on him and he flushed with the excitement that coursed through him. His arms were high, well away from his pistol.

When he felt the hand on his right shoulder, he froze, a bone-chilling fear crawling up his spine. The small hairs on the back of his neck stood straight out.

Without turning around, he glanced up into the window of the Eddy Street Saloon.

He saw the reflection.

His own . . . and the giant of a man who stood behind him.

Bolt's hand flew to his holster as he whirled around. Before he could draw his pistol, the man patted his shoulder and smiled.

"Just wanted to tell you it was a good fight," the gentleman said. "Nobody's ever stood up to Curtis Dillman and lived to tell about it."

And then the gentleman was gone.

But his words lingered in Bolt's mind for a long, long time.

CHAPTER FOUR

After emerging from the dining room of the Cheyenne Hotel, the trio stepped over to the desk clerk's counter in the elegant lobby.

Rodney Sprague, the clerk, looked up, smiled a Bolt. He was a meek-looking man with neat clean clothes, a freshly scrubbed face. He wore his dark hair short, parted in the middle. He wore a plain gold wedding band around his finger.

"We'd like two rooms, second floor if possible," Bolt said.

Sprague turned, checked the reservation board behind him, then turned back to Bolt.

"I can give you two rooms upstairs." He pushed the register toward Bolt. "Just sign your names." That's when he noticed Lena Russel, who was standing behind Bolt. His face blushed crimson. He avoided looking directly at Lena.

Bolt signed the register, pushed it over to Tom to sign. When he looked at the desk clerk, he noticed his red face, saw that the man was toying nervously with the wedding band on his finger.

"Good evening, Mr. Sprague," Lena said, her voice edged with a low husk.

"Evening, ma'am," Sprague said without looking at her. "Will you be needing a room, too?"

"Thanks, no," she said. "I won't be staying."

Bolt noticed a look of relief cross Sprague's face, a slight sigh. It was obvious that Mr. Sprague was one of the married men who visited Lena's bordello on the quiet. He was extremely uncomfortable in her presence.

"You must be the one who took . . . uh . . . Miss Russel to vote," Sprague said to Bolt. "I heard all about it."

"Just doin' my civic duty," Bolt said.

"And I heard about the fight between you and Curt Dillman. That one's a mean one, he is. Never heard of nobody yet who tangled with him and walked away alive. Pardon me for saying so, but you don't look big enough or strong enough to take on the likes of Dillman."

"Just lucky, I guess." Bolt smiled. But the hackles on the back of his neck rose again.

"Damned lucky, I'd say. Why Dillman's got to be the meanest man in Cheyenne besides his boss, Jack Sanders. Them two make quite a pair."

"Anyplace to get a bath around here?" Bolt asked, changing the subject.

"End of the hall. There's a bath room for all of our customers. Other than that, there's only one room upstairs that has its own private bath. A wooden tub. But it'll cost you a pretty penny. It's actually two rooms and the bath. It's got a separate bedroom and a sitting room."

"I'll take it," Bolt said as he pulled out his wallet. "How much?"

"It's five bucks a night. Hot water's extra if you want to use the tub."

"Yes, I want bath water. How much altogether?"

"Two buckets, two bits," said Sprague. "We have to heat the water on the cookstove in the kitchen, haul it up to the room."

"I'll take four buckets," Bolt said. "Can you have those sent up right away?" He placed five dollars and fifty cents on the counter, shoved it over to the clerk.

"Just as soon as we can heat the water. Thank you, Mr. . . ." He glanced down at the register. "Mr. Bolt. Do you want the room just for one night?"

"That's good for a starter. I'll let you know in the morning if I want it for another night."

The clerk glanced down at the register again, then looked at Tom.

"Sorry we don't have another room with a bath for you, Mr. Penrod."

"At that price, I'll bathe in my own spit," Tom grumbled.

"Hell, you'd bathe in your own piss to save a buck," Bolt laughed.

Sprague's face contorted. His body shuddered at the image Bolt's words dredged up. He turned away quickly, reached for the room keys which were in the cubby holes of the reservation board.

Tom winked at Bolt. They had a live one going and he couldn't refrain from continuing the senseless prattle.

"Yair, I probably would," Tom chided, "but that's not half as bad as the time we drank the coffee you made out of horse piss when we ran out of water."

"Gentlemen, please!" said Sprague when he faced them again. There was a pale green tint to his face. "Do you . . . do you need help with your luggage?"

"Nope," said Bolt. "Only got the one bag. Of course, I'm only speaking for myself. My friend here carries two bags." Bolt waited for Mr. Sprague to look at Tom, then stepped up closer to the counter, and spoke to the clerk in a loud whisper. "He has to carry extra clothes. You see, he wets his pants a lot."

"Oh, my," said the clerk, more flustered than he was before.

"I heard that," Tom said, mocking anger. "At least I've never burned an entire hotel down like you did by your careless smoking habits. Oh, I admit, I've set a couple of mattresses smouldering a couple of times, but nothing serious."

"Oh, dear," said Sprague nervously. "You gentlemen must be careful. The Cheyenne is a very elegant hotel and we must all do our part to keep it that way for the pleasure of future customers."

"Yes, sir, we will," said Bolt with a straight face.

"I just hope that Dillman feller doesn't come here huntin' you down. Or that Mr. Sanders. That would be even worse. We do have our rules, you know." Rodney Sprague straightened himself up, took on the position of authority again.

"What might those be?" Tom asked.

"Absolutely no fighting, either in your room or anywhere within the hotel. No women in your room after ten p.m.," he said, glancing sheepishly at Lena Russel, "unless ye be man and wife. And no harmonica playing during the quiet hours. Of course that goes for any other musical instrument that is loud."

"I play a comb," Tom said with a serious face, "does that count?"

Sprague stared at him with a blank expression for a moment.

"If you play it soft," he finally said, "I don't suppose it would bother the other customers. Here are your keys. Please have a pleasant stay at the Cheyenne Hotel."

Bolt took his key, picked up his satchel and headed for the stairs with Lena by his side, Tom following behind them. Like Bolt, he carried only one piece of luggage.

"You boys shouldn't have teased Mr. Sprague like that," Lena said when they reached the upstairs hallway. "He's a very sensitive man."

"A little kidding's good for the soul," Bolt said. "He

41

takes life too seriously."

"Henpecked, if you ask me," said Tom.

"That he is," said Lena. "You should see his wife. She's a shrew, a harpie, a real bitch. That's why he comes to the Lilac House about once a month, when his wife goes out of town to visit her parents. Sometimes he uses the girls, but sometimes he just comes to sit and talk to me. He says he likes to go someplace where he isn't nagged to death. Of course his wife would literally kill him if she found out. His job as desk clerk is the only place where he can be in authority. I feel sorry for him."

"He can change," said Bolt. "Hell, anyone can change. All he has to do is put his foot down."

"Yeah," laughed Tom, "right in the middle of his wife's face."

"I think you're right, Bolt," said Lena. "The worse she could do would be to leave him and he'd probably be relieved if she did."

"Speaking of leaving," Tom said, "I know the two of you want the pleasure of my charming company, but you'll have to make it through the evening without me. I'm gonna dump my bag in my room, change my shirt and light a shuck for the nearest saloon. See what kind of trouble I can get into."

"We all know what you want to get into, Tom," Bolt said. "Something warm and cuddly."

"Let's just say I'm going out to buy a harmonica. Always did want to learn to play one of those damned things."

"I'm sure that would please Mr. Sprague no end."

"Especially if I practice during the quiet hours."

"All kidding aside, Tom, I'd be damned careful where I went tonight. Likely there'll be a lot of drunks spoiling for a fight. Election nights are notorious for drunken brawls."

"Why, Bolt, I didn't know you cared."

"I don't. Just don't come crying to me when you get your face pounded to a pulp."

"Look who's talking about fighting. You didn't see me up there on that porch messin' with that big, strong ox." Tom unlocked his door, stepped inside the room, then stuck his head back out. "Sleep tight."

Bolt smiled and shook his head. He unlocked the door to his room, stepped inside and lit the lantern that was on a table near the door.

"Do you fellows always bicker like that?" Lena asked.

"Always. Ever since I threw a little wooden toy soldier at him at the church nursery when we were two years old."

"You've known him that long?"

"Yes. But he started it. He pulled my hair first, then I threw the toy at him."

"You seem very close." Lena's blue eyes turned sad as she lowered her head.

"Yeah, we are. We've been through a hell of a lot together."

"I've never had a friend like that, one I could talk to and kid with." She was quiet for a long moment, then she lifted her head, breathed a big sigh. "Well, I must be going now."

"Going? Where?"

Lena was still standing in the doorway, not allowing herself to step inside Bolt's room.

"Back home. To my house. But . . . but, I'm really afraid to walk home alone. I was wondering . . . I mean . . . I know you don't want to be out on the streets tonight, but I wondered if you could . . . could walk me home. I'm really scared." She was on the verge of tears.

"You're not going anyplace. You're gonna stay right

here and take a bath."

Lena started to open her mouth to protest, but Bolt didn't give her a chance. He took her hand, pulled her inside the room and closed the door, locked it. "You haven't looked in the mirror lately, have you?"

"No, but . . ."

"Your pretty face is smudged with dirt. A warm bath will do wonders for you. Hell, why do you think I paid so much extra for a room with a bath? Not for myself, for God's sake. Like Tom, I'd rather bathe with spit or piss than pay such outrageous prices."

"But, I . . ."

"Have no choice in the matter. There's no way I'm going to let you go to your own place tonight. Not with Dillman and Sanders on the rampage. Can you imagine how Sanders is gonna feel when he knows that you've already voted? Oh, I'm sure he knows by now. No, you're gonna stay right here tonight. Luckily this place has a separate bedroom. You can sleep in the bed and I'll sleep on the couch."

"No! I couldn't let you give up your bed. Not after you paid all that money."

"All right, we'll both sleep in the bed." His lips curled to a lewd smile.

"Mister Bolt! What would Rodney Sprague say?" Her blue eyes twinkled as she locked her gaze into Bolt's.

"So, I sleep on the couch." He smiled, shrugging his shoulders. "No harm in trying."

"But . . . but . . . I can't sleep here. I don't have my nightgown."

"Hell, haven't you ever slept in the buff before?"

"Buff?"

"In the raw. In the nude."

"Oh. No, I haven't."

"Try it. You might like it."

Lena looked up at Bolt as he lit another lamp on the other side of the large sitting room. There was something about his rugged face that tore at her heart. He wasn't particularly handsome in the way she had always thought of men being handsome, but he was very masculine, very exciting. His dark hair was rather long and shaggy, but she liked the way it fell naturally on his head, around his ears, nearly to his shoulders in the back. She liked the way it waved in the front, the small lock of hair that always seemed to fall on his forehead. He was tall, six feet, at least, but it was the way he carried himself that impressed her. He stood tall, sure of himself. She could picture the muscles beneath his shirt. And she couldn't trust herself to gaze into his eyes too often. They were the bluest blue she had ever seen. She even liked the way his lips curled into a sensuous smile.

Bolt blew the match out, turned the wick down. He glanced over at her.

"Yes. I might," she stammered.

"Might what?"

"Like to sleep 'in the buff,' as you say."

Bolt laughed. "You're a little slow. That was five minutes ago." He walked into the next room, the bedroom, to light a lantern, check it out.

Lena thought about it. Sleeping in the nude. She imagined herself crawling in between fresh clean sheets, the soft cloth caressing her bare flesh, clinging to her mounds, her curves. It would be a light floating sensation, a soft touch. She wouldn't let herself think about having a man next to her nude body. She knew that some people thought of her as a loose woman because she ran a bordello, but it wasn't true. She'd only known one man in her entire life and he was gone now. Dead and buried more than a year ago.

"The clerk was right," Bolt said as he came out of the

bedroom and the bathroom adjoining it. "This is a nice set up."

"Is it?"

Bolt looked at Lena. She was still standing by the door, motionless, as if she was afraid to move. Her eyes were blank, staring straight ahead as if she were in a daze.

"Lena? You all right?"

"Yes . . . yes. I'm all right. I was just thinking, that's all."

"Anything you want to talk about?"

"No. I'm just a little scared."

He walked over to her and put his hands on her shoulders. He felt her body tremble.

"There's nothing to be frightened of now. I'm here. I won't let anything happen to you."

"But what about tomorrow? We can't stay locked up in this room forever. Curt Dillman was furious. He's got a mean temper and now you've humiliated him in front of all those men. He won't forget it."

"It wasn't my intention to humiliate him. I fought a good fight and he knows it. He almost had me a couple of times. You're right, though. He'll come after me, just to save face."

Lena shuddered.

"What worries me," she said, "is that I don't think he'll wait until tomorrow to hunt you down. I think he'll take care of it tonight while the town's full of election celebrations."

Bolt took her in his arms, pulled her close. He felt her full breasts press into his chest. A twinge of desire stabbed at his loins as he held her close. He tipped her chin up with his hand, looked into her eyes for a long time. Her lips drew him to her like a magnet.

He kissed her, tenderly at first, sliding his tongue inside the warmth of her mouth. His kiss turned hard

46

and forceful as his passion increased.

He was just ready to feel a breast with his roving hand when he heard the noise out in the hall.

An instant later, there was a loud knock on the door.

Lena jumped a foot.

"I told you he wouldn't wait until tomorrow," she said, her voice filled with terror.

Bolt's hand automatically flew to his holstered pistol.

CHAPTER FIVE

Bolt motioned for Lena to move back against the far wall. He slid his pistol from the holster, took careful, quiet steps toward the door, quickly stepped to one side so he wouldn't be directly in front of the door.

The knock came again. Louder this time.

"Mr. Bolt?" the voice boomed.

"Who is it?" Bolt called.

"Your bath water, sir."

Bolt took a deep breath, slipped his pistol back in the holster. He opened the door cautiously, saw the two men standing in the hall. Each carried two buckets of steaming water. Bolt opened the door wider, let them in the room.

"That was quick," he said.

"Yes, sir," said one of the men. "Mr. Sprague said you was wantin' it right away so we stole the water the cook was heatin' fer the dirty dishes." He smiled, exposing a mouthful of crooked teeth, gaps where there should have been teeth.

"Thanks," said Bolt. "Just dump it in the tub."

"Yes, sir." The two men disappeared from the room, came back a few minutes later with empty buckets.

Bolt gave them each a generous tip, then closed and locked the door behind them.

"Ready for your bath?" Bolt asked Lena.

"Yes, but it doesn't seem fair. You should be the one to use the bath water. I mean, you paid extra for it."

"We could take a bath together." He grinned, his lips sensual and stretching to one side.

"We could," she said, smiling coyly at him. "But we

won't. I'll hurry though so you can have the bath while it's still warm."

Lena walked into the elegant bedroom, where she sat down in a hand-carved wooden chair.

"This bedroom is beautiful," she called in to Bolt. "I can see why it's so expensive. It must have cost them a fortune to furnish it." She removed her high-button shoes and stockings, placed them on the floor beside the chair. She stood up and started to unbutton the bodice of her long brown dress when she looked up and saw Bolt standing in the doorframe.

"Yes, quite beautiful, and so are you."

Lena smiled at him, held the bodice of her dress together with one hand. She made it quite clear that she didn't intend to remove her clothes with Bolt staring at her.

"I'll light the lamps in the bath room," he said. He walked into the bathroom that adjoined the bedroom, lit the lantern that was on a small wooden table near the door. Then he walked across the room, lit the hand-painted lantern that rested on a long vanity, a dressing table, complete with a mirror and padded chair.

The round tub that held the steaming water was in the middle of the room. A clothes rack with several hooks stood in a corner, beside the vanity. Original designs had been etched into the fine wood and it was polished to a shine. Two fluffy towels and washcloths were draped across a bar on another wall. Two sparkling white shelves above the towel bar displayed every type of bath aid and medicant that one would need in a year. A large house plant with bright green leaves was the finishing touch to the plush bath room. It stood near the doorway, on a porcelain pedestal.

"It's all yours," said Bolt as he came back into the bedroom.

"Thanks." Still clutching her bodice together, she went into the next room. She didn't bother to close the door between the two rooms.

"What a bathroom!" she exclaimed. "This is what I call living uptown! They even have bath oils and powders. And Polo soap! Here's some liniment. I could use that on my bruises." She rummaged through the shelves, reading the labels. "This is like having a whole drugstore at your disposal. Hotstetter's Stomach Bitters, Dr. Kilmer's Female Remedy."

"You try those bitters and you won't need anything else," Bolt laughed. "That stuff is laced with fifty percent alcohol."

"Maybe that's what I need," she said. "This room is so elegant. It gives me some ideas for decorating the Lilac House." She paused, then her voice became sad. "Except I guess I don't own the Lilac House anymore. Not since Jack Sanders took it over this morning."

"You'll get it back."

"I don't think so. You don't know Jack Sanders. He's wanted to get his hands on my bordello for a long time. He's so mean that everybody in town is afraid of him and his men. Nobody will help me get it back."

"I'm not afraid of him." Bolt sat down on the edge of the bed, on top of the thick comforter that served as a bedspread. From there he could see the round wooden bath tub, part of the vanity, the mirror above it. He could hear Lena moving about, but could not see her. He felt like he was talking to the wall. "What about the lawmen? The sheriff?"

"They won't help me," she said, a cutting edge to her voice. "It's a known fact that the sheriff and his deputies are on Jack's payroll. I've been lucky to hold onto the Lilac House as long as I have."

Still clothed, Lena walked across the small room, a towel and washcloth draped over her arm. She carried a bottle of bath oils in one hand, a bar of Polo soap in the other. She set the bath oil and soap on the dressing table, then hung the towel and washcloth on a hook on the clothes rack. She started to unbutton her dress the rest of the way down.

Bolt could see her now, but she didn't turn to look at him.

"Sounds like you and I will have to get it back then," Bolt said as he watched her.

"Oh, no, I couldn't let you do that," she said. "It's too dangerous. I was shocked when I saw you get into it with Curt Dillman. Nobody stands up to Curt the way you did. Weren't you afraid?" She slipped the dress down off her shoulders, let it slide down her body, then stepped out of it. Wearing a white slim petticoat and a lace camisole, she stepped over to the clothes rack, hung her dress on a hook.

"Didn't have time to be," Bolt said, fascinated by the slimness of her body, the fullness of her breasts beneath the camisole.

"Aren't you ever afraid of anything?" she asked. She slid the camisole up over her head, exposing her creamy white breasts.

"Of course I'm scared at times. But I don't let fear run my life. I don't run away from things. It's easier to face 'em at the time." He saw that her breasts were firm enough to stand out, despite their fullness.

"I wish I could be that way. My legs were shaking so bad when I was voting, I didn't think they'd hold me up. Sometimes I'm afraid for someone else. Like now. I'm afraid Sanders will be cruel to the girls who worked for me. Especially when he finds out I voted."

Lena slipped her petticoat down over her hips, let it slide to the floor, then stepped out of it. A minute later, she stepped out of her white panties, hung the clothing on the clothes rack.

The lamp light flickered across her body, casting a golden light across her bare flesh. Bolt watched her from the next room as she moved gracefully about. He saw the flatness of her tummy, her rounded hips, her

51

thin waistline. He saw the dark thatch of hair between her legs. In the light, it looked golden and inviting.

Desire tugged at Bolt's loins. He felt a twinge in his manhood as it began to swell. His heart beat a little faster as he felt a warm rush flood through his body.

Lena stepped over to the wooden tub, dipped her hand down to test the water. Satisfied that it was not too hot, she walked over to the vanity, picked up the small bottle she had found on the shelf, carried it to the tub. She removed the lid, poured some of the contents into the tub, then splashed the water until bubbles formed. As she leaned over, her full breasts bounced up and down. She took the bottle of bath oils back to the vanity, picked up the bar of Polo soap, stripped off the paper wrapping that proclaimed the soap a product of Procter & Gamble. On her way back to the tub with the soap, she snatched the washcloth from the hook.

The lavender scent of the bath oils floated in the air to the bedroom where it attacked Bolt's already aroused senses. He took a deep breath, felt his swelling manhood throb against the confining material of his trousers. As Lena stepped into the tub, he caught a glimpse of the pink flesh of her pussy. He shifted positions as he sat on the edge of the bed, trying to give his bulging cock more room in the restraining trousers.

"How did you come to own the Lilac House?" he asked, a new husk to his voice. He cleared his throat before continuing. "Did your father own it before he died?"

"Oh heavens no! He'd probably turn over in his grave if he knew I owned a bordello." Her voice became muffled as she lathered the washcloth and scrubbed her face and neck. "No, after he died, I didn't know how I was going to make it. He wasn't wealthy but he thought he had enough life insurance to take care of me if anything happened to him. As it turned out, he didn't have anything. The insurance agent turned out to be a crook. He pocketed my father's insurance premiums and issued him a phony insurance policy. The insurance company wouldn't honor my claim because they stated they never received any of the premium payments. Naturally, the agent skipped town and I ended up without a dime." As she scrubbed her arms, she winced in pain when she touched the bruises Jack Sanders had inflicted on her.

"I'm sorry to hear that."

"I didn't know what to do," she continued. "I lost Papa's house because I couldn't keep up the mortgage payments. I had no one to turn to, no kin close enough to contact. There aren't any jobs for women unless you're a school teacher and I wasn't qualified for that. When I got real desperate, I decided I'd have to become a prostitute just to earn money for food and shelter. It was all that was left for me to do. I went to the Lilac House to apply for a job because it was the nicest whorehouse in town. I felt guilty because I thought Papa was watching over me from beyond the grave. I'm sure he visited the Lilac House on several occasions before he died. He was so lonesome. Anyway, I got the job right away because I was still a virgin."

While she bathed, she continued to chatter as if she were talking to herself, as if she had to get it out in the open to ease her guilt. She dipped the washcloth into the water, wrung it out and draped it over the side of the tub.

Bolt watched as she took the soap in her hands, rubbed it to a lather. She let the soap slip back into the water, then moved her hands to her breasts. She rubbed her slippery, soapy hands all over the large breasts, massaging them until they were covered with bubbly lather. God, he thought, didn't she know what she was doing to him. His manhood throbbed against the tightness of his Levi's. He unbuttoned his fly. He meant only to ease the pressure on his swollen member.

53

His cock snapped to attention, causing his shorts to become a pointed cloth tent.

While still sitting down, he pushed his shorts down so that his cock jutted straight out in the air, free of the confining material. He didn't speak to Lena. He didn't trust the husk in his voice.

"My very first customer," she continued, "was a very nice older gentleman. He was very gentle with me and after we made love, he said he didn't want me to work in that profession anymore. He was a wealthy cattle rancher and he offered me enough money so I wouldn't have to be a prostitute. I told him I couldn't accept his money. He wasn't married and he offered to let me live at his ranch for nothing, but I couldn't do that either. So, he bought the Lilac House for me, told me I could run it and pay him back the money from the profits. He never came back to the bordello again as a customer, but of course we saw a lot of each other after that. Fact is, we were planning to marry. Unfortunately, he was killed in a tragic accident about a year ago. Gored to death by a wild bull. So I kept the Lilac House and it's been good to me. But now, I just don't know . . ."

She rinsed the soap suds from her breasts by dipping her hands into the bath water, letting the water drip down over the breasts. The rivulets of water glimmered off the bare flesh, dripped from the nipples.

Her hands found the soap again. After rubbing it between her palms for a moment, she moved one hand below the water level, placed it between her legs. She moved her hand in a circular motion.

Bolt watched her profile as she tipped her head back, closed her eyes. Her mouth fell open then closed slightly to form a small O. She was beautiful as the flickering lamp etched her fine facial features into a painting.

Her hand continued to move in a slow circular

motion beneath the water. Above the water, her long dark hair cascaded down her back in stark contrast to her alabaster skin. Her tongue protruded from her puckered mouth, ran sensuously across her lips.

Bolt's imagination went wild. It was more than he could stand. His bare cock pulsed with a hunger that needed to be satisfied.

He removed his clothes quickly, silently. Without making a sound, he moved into the bathroom. Like a panther stalking his prey. Standing beside the tub, he saw that her eyes were still closed, her lips wet and inviting as her tongue traced its sensual path.

He leaned over, bent his head down, drawn to her lips like a magnet. His lips touched her in a blaze of fire. He slid his tongue inside her damp mouth, flicked at her tongue.

She did not back away. She responded with her own passion, drawing his tongue deep inside her mouth.

Holding her head with both hands, he kissed her passionately, pressing hard against her full lips.

As he stepped into the warm water, she opened her eyes, looked up at him with her own hunger.

He kissed her again with wild passion. He wanted her very much. His hand slid down to her wet, slippery breast. He cupped it in his hand, massaged it, felt the nipple harden under his touch. He wanted her even more.

He drew her hand out of the water, placed it on his protruding cock. The sensation of her warm, wet hand on his organ was overpowering. His cock throbbed and pulsed in her hand.

As he eased himself down into the warm water, he knew it was too late to back away now.

He had to have her.

Even if she resisted, he had to take her.

It was the only way to satisfy the deep hunger he had.

CHAPTER SIX

The water churned with their passionate antics.

Bolt kissed her, crushing her lips with his lust. His hand slid into the water, stroked her pussy. He liked the feel of her slippery body and couldn't keep his hands from roaming her body, stopping to play with her silky breasts, tweak the nipples to hardness. He tried to get her in a position where he could penetrate her, but found the tub too small and confining to accomplish the feat.

Frustrated, he stood up. Before he could pull her to a standing position, she grabbed the soap, lathered both hands, then reached for his swollen cock. She slid her soapy hands along the length of it, squeezing gently as she did.

The warmth of her hands, the slippery feel of the suds, made him want her even more. When he thought he could stand it no more, she splashed his body with the bath water, rinsing the soap away. She was still sitting in the tub and the way he was standing above her, his dripping cock was just inches away from her mouth.

She leaned forward, kissed the tip end.

A shot of desire stabbed at his loins. His body shuddered with the pleasure that coursed through him.

She took the stiff cock into her mouth, sheathing it with warm saliva. It twiched in her mouth as Bolt struggled to keep from exploding his seed. She suckled on it, ran her tongue around the mushroomed head, attacked the slit eye with a probing tongue. She wrapped her hand around the base of his cock, took it deep inside her mouth until it touched the back of her throat. She withdrew it slowly, sucking so hard her cheeks caved in. She moved her mouth back and forth along its length with increased speed until he was about to spill his seed.

He grabbed her, pulled her to a standing position. He drew her close and kissed her again. Their dripping bodies crushed against each other. He moved around until his rock-hard cock slipped between her damp legs. He felt her legs tighten around his pulsing organ as he reached around behind her, grabbed her fleshy buttocks and drew her even closer.

"I want you," he husked. "Now."

"Take me."

He stepped out of the tub, snatched a towel from the rack. He threw it around his shoulders, then got the other towel for her. He dried himself quickly, tossed the towel at the rack.

"Let me dry you off," he said, taking her towel from her. He rubbed her back briskly with the fluffy towel, turned her around and dabbed at her shoulders, her tummy. He took longer to dry her breasts, her furry mound between her legs. He tossed her towel back over his shoulder.

Cupping one of her ample breasts in his hands, he lowered his head, took a nipple into his mouth. He flicked his tongue across it until it became hard and rubbery. He suckled on it like a newborn babe, massaged the pliant flesh.

Suddenly, he scooped her up in his arms, carried her to the next room and tossed her gently on the bed.

She scrambled between the sheets, pulled the top sheet and comforter up around her neck. She looked up at him with teasing eyes.

"You'll have to find me first," she giggled.

"Woman, you're gonna get fucked like you never been fucked before." He ripped the covers back, scrambled up on the bed beside her.

"I hope so," she husked as he positioned himself above her. She spread her legs wide to accept him.

He lowered himself, found her damp pussy with his throbbing probe. He slid his cock along her slippery slit, then gave a gentle push. He penetrated the folds of her sex with no effort. With one thrust, he slid deep inside her warm honeypot.

She moaned and squirmed with pleasure as he rocked her with his rapid, deep strokes. Her hips undulated as she rose and fell to match his rhythm.

He felt her muscles tighten around his rigid organ every time he started to withdraw his cock. It was as if she was trying to hold him deep inside her. The pressure sent a new thrill through him every time she tightened up.

His flesh slapped against hers as he pumped into her sex. Faster and faster. Deeper and deeper. There was no stopping him. No slowing him down. He wanted to make their sex last forever. He wanted to ease up on his strokes, prolong what he knew was about to happen. He wanted to play with her body for hours, work himself up to the edge of ecstasy, hold back, then do it again.

But he had reached the point of no return.

He plunged into her flesh for the last time, driving in as deep as he could. He grabbed her buttocks, pulled her close, held her tight as his seed bubbled and boiled, spilled out. For a brief instant, his mind was void of everything except for a fusion of pure joy, ultimate ecstasy. His heart pounded in his chest as he caught his breath. It took a few moments before he found the strength to roll off of her.

"You're some kind of man," Lena said after a few minutes.

"And you're quite a lady." He smiled.

"You did things to me . . . I mean you touched spots that I didn't even know I had. I've never felt like this before. Oooooh, it felt so good when you put it inside me. I felt a kind of throbbing down there just after you put it inside. I don't know what it was but it felt like I was in another world. In a very special paradise." She snuggled over against his bare body.

"You keep talking like that," he said, "and I'm going to drive it home again."

"You mean you're not going to send me home?" she teased.

"Hell no. I'm going to get my money's worth out of this room." He propped himself up on his elbow, blew the lantern out, then snuggled down in bed with her.

"Is it always this good?" she asked.

"It should be," he said, "but it isn't always."

"Have you known a lot of women?"

The knock on the door startled both of them.

Bolt jumped out of bed. Not bothering with his shorts, he slipped into his Levi's, snatched the pistol from his holster which was on the floor by the bed where he had stripped out of his clothes earlier.

Lena, too frightened to move, grabbed the covers, pulled them up tight around her neck. She glanced toward the bathroom where one lamp still burned. She saw her brown dress on the clothes rack, wondered if she should run in there and get dressed. But she was paralyzed with fear, unable to move.

Bolt dashed into the sitting room. He had not blown the lantern out and the room was bathed in a flickering light.

The knock came again as he neared the door.

"Lena!" called the frantic voice beyond the door. It was a woman's voice. Shrill, insistent. "Lena! It's Brenda Loomis. I've got to talk to you!"

Lena recognized Brenda's voice. She got out of bed

quickly, went to the bathroom and took her dress from the hook. She slipped it over her head just as Bolt opened the door to the hall.

"Is Lena here?" Brenda said as she dashed into the room, walked on by Bolt. Her wide, frightened eyes darted around the room.

She was young, seventeen or eighteen, Bolt thought. She wore a scanty red outfit with long dark stockings, too much rouge on her pretty face. The traditional garment for soiled doves. He saw that her stockings were torn, her light brown hair disheveled.

"Yes, just a minute." Bolt closed the door, turned around. But he didn't have to call Lena out from the bedroom. She entered the sitting room, still buttoning her long brown dress.

"Brenda! What are you doing here?" she said as she dashed over to the young, overwrought girl.

"Oh, Lena, I've looked all over for you. When I didn't find you at your house, I figured you stayed in town. I checked at two other hotels before I came here. The desk clerk told me you were up here."

"Look at you. You're a mess. What happened?"

"It's Jack Sanders! He's at the Lilac House, claiming he's the new boss."

"I know. How bad is it?"

"Worse than you can imagine. He's invited all of his filthy cronies to the bordello to celebrate his victory in the election and they're all drunk. It's terrible!"

"Was Sanders running for public office?" Bolt asked.

"No," said Lena.

"Then what the hell does he have to celebrate? He didn't keep you from voting like he planned."

"He was instrumental in getting a proposal placed on the ballot—against woman's suffrage. He put out a lot of propaganda flyers about the issue. He wanted the law changed to revoke the right for women to vote. He

60

spread the rumor that men would be emasculated if they continued to let the women of Cheyenne vote. And he made it clear that they would risk losing protection by the local sheriff deputies if they didn't vote his way. That's why he didn't want me or any other women to vote. He knew which way I'd vote."

Bolt shook his head, turned to Brenda.

"Are the men treating you girls badly?"

"You can't believe how bad it is. Sanders is bragging to all his friends that he's treating them to what he calls 'an annual donkey dinner.'"

"What's that?" asked Lena.

"Sanders explained to his men that it's where everyone gets a free piece of ass. The men went wild with laughter, then they started chasing all of us around. They're rough and mean. Lena, you've got to do something. The girls are hysterical and I only managed to escape by climbing out of a second story window."

"Did anyone see you leave?" Bolt asked.

"No. They were all too busy slapping the girls around and raping them. I saw one drunken lecher hit Linda hard across the head, knocked her to the floor and . . . and . . . raped her right there in front of everyone. He didn't even bother to take his pants off. Just pushed them down so his fat ass was showing. The men thought it was funny, but it was horrible. I just couldn't stand it anymore!" Her body shivered with the memory.

"I'll go over there and put a stop to it," Bolt said, "even if I have to dump a little lead into one of their bellies to make my point." He went into the bedroom, grabbed his shirt, boots and holster, his hat. He took them into the sitting room where he quickly dressed.

Lena ran over to him, grabbed him by the shoulders.

"No! You can't go over there alone!" she cried. "It's

too dangerous! You'd be outnumbered! You'd be killed!"

Bolt took her hands from his shoulders, held them in his own hands.

"I have to go, Lena. I can't let that bastard Sanders and the other men mistreat the girls like that. I couldn't live with myself if I didn't do everything possible to keep those girls from being tortured."

"I'll go with you, then. I can handle a gun."

"No, you stay here. Both of you stay here. Keep the door locked. Don't let anyone in."

"But you can't go alone," she pleaded, her blue eyes wide as saucers. "I know how dangerous those men are. They have no respect for another human being's life. They'd kill you in a minute and not think anything about it. And they're not afraid of dying, either! Oh, Bolt, please don't go!" She was on the edge of hysteria.

"It's something I have to do. When I think of those poor helpless girls . . ."

"Where's Tom?" Lena cried. "He could help you."

"I don't know, but I don't have time to chase him down. I have to get those girls out of there. Now. Before anyone gets hurt bad. What Jack Sanders is doing to them is not only cruel, it's inhumane. I can't let him get away with it. If the law won't stop him then maybe I can."

"Oh, Bolt, how are you going to manage it?"

"I don't know, but I'll think of something. Does the Lilac House have a back door?"

"Yes, but . . ."

"Good. Maybe they'll be so busy they won't see me coming."

"No! It won't work! Don't you understand?"

"The only thing I understand is that Sanders and his depraved friends are torturing young innocent girls. Raping them, beating them. Maybe even killing them.

And I'm not going to stand around and let it happen if there is anything I can do to help those girls. That's what's wrong with today's society. Apathy! Nobody cares about anybody else anymore. They let corrupt men like Sanders come in and take over a town instead of stopping them before they can do any damage, before they can get so powerful that nobody can fight them. The general public just doesn't care about these things. Not unless it affects them directly. Not until one of their loved ones gets hurt or killed. Do you understand what I'm trying to say?"

Lena batted her eyes, tried to fight back the tears that welled up in her eyes.

"Yes, I understand," she said softly. "That's how I felt about voting this morning. There were other women who wanted to vote, but I felt I had to make the stand to protect our rights."

"Then you know why I have to go."

"I know. I just don't know why it has to be you," she said. "Why do you have to go?"

Bolt shook his head. Lena had missed his point. "For the same reason that it had to be you who voted this morning."

She looked up at him with sad eyes. A tear drop spilled over, trickled down her cheek. He thought she finally understood.

Bolt checked his pistol, shoved it into his holster, walked toward the door.

"Don't go! You'll get killed!" Lena screamed as he opened the door.

He stepped out in the hall, closed the door behind him, waited until he heard Lena secure the bolt from the inside. He walked toward the stairway, Lena's words still ringing in his ears.

He hoped they weren't prophetic.

CHAPTER SEVEN

Cheyenne was a rip-roaring place that election night. Tom Penrod had seen more drunken fights during the past hour than he'd seen in a month of Sundays. He was beginning to wish he'd taken Bolt's advice and stayed holed up in his room for the duration of the victory celebrations. Only problem with that was that Bolt had a pretty young thing in his room while Tom himself was left with an empty bed and a basic human urge that needed filling.

Tom had seen more than one drunken fighter hauled away to the hoosegow by local lawmen. But a new fight errupted every few minutes and there just weren't enough local peace officers to handle the situation. Tom had avoided the roudiest saloons where the customers shouted and shoved each other and drank the hard whiskey until the tempers flared and the arguments began.

He had no desire to get thrown into jail with a bunch of drunks. He imagined the facilities at the jail would be a bit crowded tonight and more than a little smelly.

Avoiding the rowdy saloons, Tom found a small place off the beaten track. Called Harry's Poker Parlor, the tavern had a long bar along the back wall, a billiard table off to one side, several tables and chairs. The place was crowded and noisy with the excitement of the election, but at least the men customers seemed to be a little less unruly than others he'd seen that night. He'd been there for almost an hour and he'd only seen one fight. Two men who had been drinking since early afternoon finally got into an argument about how many stars were on the flag. They exchanged a couple of punches, but Harry Potter, the owner, had escorted them outside before they could do any damage to his saloon.

The air in Harry's Poker Parlor was close, stifling, full of cigarette smoke and whiskey fumes. The noise was just as stifling, ear-shattering, as boisterous customers became louder to be heard above the sound of the tinkling piano, the female singer. In a vicious circle, the piano player plunked harder, the vocalist sang louder to be heard above the din of the crowd.

Tom didn't know what was so special about an election night that grown men felt they had to overindulge in rot-gut whiskey and stale beer and make fools of themselves. He figured it was more an excuse to drink than anything else. Maybe they needed an excuse to get a brief respite from the pressures of their labors, the tough times.

Tom sat alone at a corner table near the piano. He sat with his back against the wall so he could see the entertainers and yet watch the rowdy customers at the same time. He wasn't looking for trouble, or expecting it. That's why he had chosen the table away from the majority of the customers. If another fight broke out, he'd be far enough away so that he wouldn't get hurt in the melee.

He sipped his whiskey, enjoyed watching the different personalities emerge from generally decent men as the booze took effect. He didn't care so much about the drink in front of him. He had come to the saloon to find a glitter gal to spend some time with. He had come to feed the animal lust that burned deep in his loins. But it was a busy night for everyone. All of the soiled doves were in use at the moment and he had to wait his turn. He didn't mind waiting. It had been a long, hard ride from Denver and he was ready for a good woman.

Carmen Olay's voice became louder, more shrill as the singer tried to be heard above the hubbub of the crowded saloon. She glanced down at Tom and smiled, shook her head.

Sympathizing with her, Tom smiled back, shrugged his shoulders. He took another sip of his drink, stared at her over the brim of his glass.

Carmen Olay was an attractive woman with a plain face. Not really pretty, but earthy in the way she sang, the way she moved her body when she sang. With her long dark hair, high cheekbones and dark complexion, she looked part Spanish. She wore a long red dress that clung to her full, mature figure and Tom guessed her to be in her late twenties.

As the noise level of the saloon increased, so did Miss Olay's singing. She had a pleasant voice until she strained it to be heard. She looked directly at Tom while she sang the last notes of a ballad. When she finished the song, she gave it up for a lost cause.

Tom smiled at her, applauded.

Carmen strolled over to his table.

"Thanks," she said. "I think you're the only one who was listening."

"It was nice, what I could hear of it," Tom laughed. "Care to sit down?"

Carmen glanced at the empty chair across from Tom.

"You waiting for someone?"

"Not exactly." Tom grinned.

"I know what you're saying," said Carmen as she slid into the chair. "But you've got a long wait ahead of you, Mr. . . . ah . . ."

"Penrod. Call me Tom."

"Tom Penrod," she said as if testing the sound of it.

66

"I like the name. You new in town?"

"Just rode in this afternoon. Can I buy you a drink?"

"No thanks. I won't be staying that long. I'm going home and change out of this tight dress. I guess I should lose a few pounds."

"You look fine just the way you are, Carmen."

"Ah, you're a true gentleman." She leaned back in her chair, studied Tom with her dark brown eyes.

"Looks like I picked the wrong night to come to town."

"You sure did. Those girls are working their asses off, if you'll pardon the expression. It's been like this since early afternoon. There's gotta be a mile-long waiting list for their services. Makes me glad I sing for my supper. The pay's not great, but I'd be plumb tuckered out if I had to put on a smile and be nice to all those drunks."

"Yair, I reckon that could wear a person out." Without taking his eyes off of Carmen's animated face, Tom took another sip of his whiskey. He liked her spunk, her openness.

"I wonder what makes men act like fools on election night," Carmen said. "Normally these men are pretty decent. Quiet and orderly. Not that I mind the fellers having a good time, but when they start to shout and argue, it scares the hell out of me. One of 'em's likely to pull a knife or a gun as not. You seem to be the only sane one here!"

"I didn't vote." Tom smiled.

"I didn't either. Not that I didn't want to, but there's no way I was gonna risk my fanny by showing up at the polls. Not with Jack Sanders and his filthy bunch so opposed to women voting. Far as I know there was only one woman brave enough to vote today. And I hear she went through hell before she finally got to cast her ballot. Seems a couple of strangers finally took her

67

back to the polls and stood guard while she voted. They even had to stand up to one of Sanders' men. I hear it was quite a fight."

"It was," Tom said.

"Oh, were you there?" She looked at him closer. "Were you . . . are you? Yes! You're one of the strangers, aren't you?"

"There are some who consider me a stranger," Tom laughed. "But I wasn't the one who tangled with Curt Dillman, if that's what you're thinking."

"You're not?" Carmen seemed disappointed.

"Nope. It was my friend. Jared Bolt."

"I knew it! I knew it!" she beamed. "You are one of the strangers who helped Lena Russel vote! Well, I take my hat off to you and your friend. I wish there were more like you around. Maybe the rest of us women could have voted then."

"Maybe if you had all banded together, you could have voted. Nothing more frightening to a man than a bunch of wet hens."

"Wouldn't have worked. All of the women around here are afraid of Sanders' shadow. Half the men, too."

"Why don't you kick the bum out of town?"

"He's too powerful. Nobody will buck him."

"A man can't get powerful unless others allow him to."

Carmen looked at Tom for a long time. Her respect for him was increasing all the time.

"You know, you're right. We, the townspeople, have allowed Sanders and his mob to intimidate us. We've allowed him to become powerful. But how do we change things at this late date?"

"By changing yourselves, your attitudes. As long as everybody fears Sanders, he will be powerful. Once people begin changing and lose their fear of him, he will lose his power."

"Sounds simple the way you put it. But it will take a long time to make things better, won't it?"

"Probably. Things didn't get bad overnight."

"I wonder if the time will ever come when women can just go to the polling places and vote without being harassed by men."

"It'll come, but like other changes, it'll take some attitude adjustments. And time."

"You're absolutely right. I like you, Tom."

"Even if I'm a stranger?" He grinned.

"Because you're strange," she laughed. "The noise in here is shattering my ear drums and the smoke is enough to gag a maggot. Think I'll call it a night. Would you like to come home with me and have a drink where it's quiet enough to talk?"

"Where's home?" Tom asked when he wanted to ask who else was at home, if there was a jealous husband waiting for her.

"I live right next door, at the Lodgepole Hotel . . . alone. You're welcome to come over for a drink . . . unless you want to stay here and play the waiting game."

Tom didn't know whether that was an invitation or a proposition. Her offer seemed casual enough, but the expression in her eyes said more than her words.

"Sounds ideal to me. I don't like crowds anyway."

"Good." She reached across the table, put her hand on his. There was a twinkle in her big brown eyes. "Besides, why pay for something when you can get it for free?"

Tom knew now that it was a proposition.

He stood up, walked around the table and pulled Carmen's chair out while she got up. He looked more closely at her full figure in the tight red gown. She might think she was a bit overweight, but for him, she was just perfect. He liked a little meat on the bones.

There'd be a little more to get his hands on.

They were halfway across the crowded saloon when a shadow crossed their paths. Tom sensed trouble before he looked up from Carmen's flared behind.

Curt Dillman stood directly in their path, his hands jammed on his hips. He towered over Tom by a good four inches. He glared down at Tom with a smug look, arrogantly stretching his tall frame even taller.

Tom started to push his way around the big man.

Dillman reached out with one long arm, shoved Tom backwards.

Carmen screamed.

Heads turned in their direction as the customers at Harry's Poker Parlor craned their necks to see what had caused the shrill scream. There were shouts of confusion at first as the men jostled each other in an attempt to get a better view. Gradually the voices faded away into silence.

Tom regained his balance, straightened up to stand in front of Dillman again. His hand hovered above his holster.

Dillman didn't go for his pistol. Instead, he raised his hands to his chest, hooked his thumbs into his suspenders. One of his eyes was puffy, swollen to a slit. The skin around the eye was ugly and purple. Under his other eye, a jagged cut ran diagonally across his cheek and another fresh cut traced a path along the opposite chin bone. All evidence of Bolt's handiwork earlier that afternoon.

"Seems to me we have some business to settle up, stranger," Dillman said, his words slightly slurred. He stretched his suspenders out, let them snap back in place.

"I don't have any business with you, mister," Tom said, standing his ground.

The men in the saloon began to move back away

from the two men, giving them a wide berth. Except for the shuffle of feet, the hushed whispers, the room became quiet as the tension rippled through the crowd.

Carmen backed away, bumped into a chair and knocked it over. She felt behind her with her hands, searched for a table that would give her support. Her brown eyes were wide with fear.

"Yes, you do," said Dillman. "You and your friend should have wiped your snotty noses instead of sticking them where they didn't belong. You shoulda kept right on riding instead of stopping in Cheyenne 'cause we don't allow no trash here. And we don't allow no whores voting. You heard the men out there today. They didn't want no women voters."

"I heard 'em laugh when you got your balls stomped," Tom said.

"Why, you dirty sonofabitch!" Dillman's hands went down to his waistline, but he still didn't go for his gun. His face flushed with anger.

Harry Potter, the owner of the saloon, heard the commotion. He came around from behind the bar, started threading his way through the crowd.

Tom waited for Dillman to make the next move.

"You'll regret what you did today the rest of your life," Dillman snarled.

"I didn't do anything to you."

"No, but your friend did. And since he ain't here, you're gonna pay for his mistakes." Dillman's body swayed with his drunkenness.

Harry Potter broke through the crowd, came up to the two men. He held his arms high in the air, waved his hands.

"Gentlemen!" Harry called. "There's no fighting allowed inside the saloon. What you do outside is your own business, but I won't let you stay in here and destroy my place. I'm asking both of you to leave right now. Settle your differences somewhere else."

"Wouldn't think of fightin' in here, Harry, and bustin' up your fucking place," Dillman slurred. "I was just gonna suggest the same thing." He turned back to Tom. "I'm invitin' you outside to finish the fight your friend started."

"I've already got an invitation," said Tom. "A better one than yours."

"I'll be waitin' outside. If you're not out there in three minutes, I'm comin' back in here and blast your balls to bloody pulp. They'll wipe up the floor with you." Dillman turned and staggered toward the door.

Nobody moved until Dillman was gone.

Carmen dashed up to Tom, looped her arms in his and squeezed it tight.

"Tom, what are you going to do?" she cried. "You can't go out there. He'll kill you!"

Tom walked over to the window, stood to one side and peeked out. The light from the saloon spilled out onto the boardwalk in front of the building, on out to the street. Tom saw Dillman standing near the door, checking his pistol. He watched as Dillman rubbed his hand over the barrel, then tested the sights, aiming it just beyond the door.

Something else caught Tom's eye. A shadow off to the left. He squinted his eyes, made out the shape of a barrel. But there was more than just the barrel. The shadow changed configurations. There was someone hiding behind the barrel. The light reflected off of something metal beside the barrel. As his eyes adjusted to the near darkness, he saw that it was a long rifle. So, Dillman was not alone.

Tom scanned the area in front of the saloon. Another shadow appeared. Near the hitchrail. He made out the shape of a man, a rifle, by the post of the rail. The form moved slightly, took aim at the door.

Looking further, Tom saw still another gunman. Beyond Dillman. Out in the street, tucked back behind a wagon.

So there were three gunmen besides Dillman out there. Dillman must have come looking for Bolt and himself and brought his reinforcements with him.

Tom walked back over to Carmen.

"You're right. I can't go out there. He'll kill me. And if he doesn't, there are three more just like him out there who will."

CHAPTER EIGHT

"You've got to do something!" Carmen said. "You can't stay here! He'll come back in here after you!"

"Have they got a back door in this place?"

"Yes. Go out the back way! Where's your friend?"

"You mean Bolt?"

"Yes. Where is he? Quick!"

"At the Cheyenne Hotel. Why?"

"I'm going to get him. You're going to need some help."

"But you can't."

"It'll work. I'll go out the front door as if I were going home. That'll distract them some."

"But it's too dangerous. They'll think it's me and there are at least four guns pointed at that door."

"I'll make sure they know it's me. I'll call out and tell them I'm leaving before the fireworks start. They'll believe it."

"No. I can't let you . . ."

"Look. Dillman won't bother me. He's after you. If there's any trouble, I'll just duck into the hotel where I'll be safe. That'll give you a chance to get out the back way before they get suspicious. By the time Dillman figures out you're not coming out, he'll come back in here after you. You'll have a little head start, but every minute will count. With four gunmen out there, it's gonna get sticky when they find out you've high-tailed it out the back way. You can bet your sweet patuta they'll come after you."

Tom took a deep breath, squeezed her hand. The

seconds ticked by. Precious seconds.

"Be careful, Carmen."

"You, too."

Tom made a dash for the back of the room, pushing the surprised men aside.

A hand fell on Tom's shoulder. He turned around, faced the man who had grabbed him.

"Why don't cha go fight the bastard?" the drunken man slurred. "You a sissy?" The drunk swayed back and forth, barely able to keep his balance.

"Fight him yourself," Tom said, freeing himself from the man's clutches. He elbowed his way through another throng of men. He heard the sarcastic remarks offered by the drunks who were in a fighting mood. He ignored them, pushed on through to the back.

At the same time, Carmen Olay walked slowly to the front door. When she reached it, she turned the knob, opened the door cautiously.

It was quiet outside. Too quiet.

Her heart pounded inside her. She knew that when she stepped through the door, there would be four guns trained on her.

She opened the door a little more. She still couldn't see Curt Dillman or any of the other men. But she knew they were there. She could feel their ominous presence. She sensed their tense muscles as they held their weapons steady on the door.

"Goodnight, Harry," she called in an overly loud voice.

"You leaving already?" Harry called back.

She was a little surprised that Harry had answered her, but it was all right. It worked into her plan.

"Hope you don't mind me leaving early, but if there's going to be a fight, I don't want to stick around."

"O.K. See you tomorrow."

She hesitated before opening the door wide. She had

made the commitment and now she had to go through with it. She pushed the door wide open. And then she saw him. Dillman was crouched down, off to her left, his pistol aimed at her head. She would have to walk right by him to go in the direction she wanted to go. She held her breath, fully expecting to be shot down in cold blood at any moment.

Dillman didn't move. He was like a statue. Cold and hard, motionless. Without heart or feeling.

She took a tentative step, then another. Dillman watched her with eagle eyes. His pistol was unwavering. She stepped out onto the boardwalk in front of the saloon, her eyes riveted on Dillman. She turned, walked in his direction. He was not more than five feet in front of her.

Bracing herself, she moved toward him at a normal walking pace. She walked right on by him, ignoring him as if he weren't there.

Dillman's pistol didn't follow her. It was still aimed at the door.

She let her breath out slow and easy. As she neared the hitching post, she spotted one of the other gunmen. She saw the long barrel of the rifle first, then the man who leaned against the post to steady his rifle. She recognized the face in the dim light. It was Brad Emmons, one of Jack Sanders' henchmen. As she walked closer, she saw that his rifle was also trained on the door instead of her.

She breathed a little easier once she had passed him. She wanted to look back. Just to be sure. But she couldn't. She appeared calm on the outside, but inside, her muscles were knotted with fear, her nerves jangling.

She should have looked around. She might have had a chance then.

A moment later, a large, cold hand clamped tight around her mouth. Fear shot through her, dumped adrenalin into her system. She tried to scream, but no sound came out. The hand bore down on her mouth, crushing her lips against her teeth.

With a rifle in one hand, Brad Emmons jerked her head around with the other. He twisted her neck, pushed it against her shoulder.

Pain racked her brain. She struggled to free herself but Emmons was strong. The more she fought him, the more he hurt her with his vicious power.

A minute later, Curt Dillman came up and stood in front of Carmen. He leered at her with cruel eyes.

"You should be more careful about the company you keep, Miss Carmen," he laughed harshly. "We don't cotton to our women takin' up with no stranger. Especially when he's a trouble-makin' bastard. Too bad you won't get a chance to spread your legs for him, but by the time we get through with you, he wouldn't want you. Ain't that right, Brad?"

"That's right, Curt. Not unless he wants seconds or thirds."

"More than that." Dillman reached over and felt Carmen's breast. He squeezed it hard in his strong hand.

Carmen winced in pain. She tried to kick Dillman in the shins, but she missed. Emmons jerked her neck again to keep her in line.

"Nice tits," said Dillman. "Big and firm." He jammed his hand down between her legs, squeezed the mound of her sex that was covered by the tight dress.

Carmen tried to open her mouth to bite Brad's finger, but the pressure from his hand was too much. She kicked backwards, stabbed at the air with her shoe. Her elbows flew back as she tried to jab them into the man's gut, but she couldn't make contact.

"Ah, we got a lively one," Dillman slurred. "Jack will love her."

77

Carmen's blood turned to ice at the mention of Jack. Jack Sanders. Curt had to be talking about Jack Sanders.

"You mean you're gonna take her over to the Lilac House?" Brad Emmons said.

"Of course."

"But I thought . . ."

"No. She's too good to waste. I'm gonna score some points with Jack by bringing Miss Carmen to the party. She's prime stuff. She'll add some spice to the party, don't cha think? Besides, the fellers are probably gettin' a little tired of stickin' it to them whores. This one's got class."

"But what about that Penrod feller?"

"That bastard'll get his. I got him covered. He can't take a step outside without gettin' blasted. Let's get goin' while the party's still young."

Carmen had never known fear like this before. It tore at her guts, made her sick to her stomach. It blinded her mind to reason, hammered at her brain until it fogged over with absolute panic. It felt like she was falling down a long dark tunnel with no bottom. She fought to stay conscious although she wished she'd faint dead away so she wouldn't have to know what was happening to her.

She prayed that Tom would get out alive.

She prayed that she was asleep, that this was one big ugly nightmare.

She felt herself being dragged down the street and she knew it was true.

Tom ran down the back hallway off the main room of the saloon. He spotted the door at the end of the hall. He hoped that Dillman was a slow counter and that he hadn't come back inside the saloon looking for him. He hoped that Carmen had made it past the gunmen without any trouble. He kept his ears trained for gunshots, but so far, so good.

He hoped that he and Carmen reached the Cheyenne Hotel at the same time and that he wouldn't need Bolt's help. He could make love to Carmen just as well in his room as hers. After the scene with Dillman in the saloon, they'd both be glad to go to bed in each other's arms.

He reached the door, turned the knob, was glad that the door wasn't locked. He opened the door, started outside.

The light from the hall lantern fanned out in rays across the ground behind the building.

Almost too late, he saw the two men. One on each side of the door frame. Both had pistols drawn.

The night air erupted with gunfire as both men fired simultaneously.

Tom had ducked back inside just in time. An instant before the triggers were squeezed. He slammed the door shut, took the hallway by leaps and bounds, his feet barely touching the floor. He didn't stop until he was back inside the main room with the crowded bar. He tried to get lost in the crowd, blend in with them so he wouldn't be noticed.

Harry Potter saw him enter the room, marched over to him.

"You can't stay here," Harry said. "I already told you that. You don't wanta fight, you go out the back door."

"But they're waitin' out there for me! I can't go out either door!"

"Well, you can't stay here!" Harry nodded to one of his employees. A minute later a big burly giant of a man came over, stood beside his boss. His arms were folded across his huge barrel chest.

"I ain't goin' out in that alley," said Tom. "You got a side window I can use?"

"No, but you better get your ass out of here. I don't aim to get my place busted up by a couple of drunks like you and Dillman. There'll be hell to pay if even one iota of my property is damaged. Now, you got the picture? Get the hell out of here!"

"But you don't understand!"

"I understand perfectly," Harry ranted. "You're a stranger in town, Mister. You think you can come in here and mix with the locals. Not that we mind strangers here, mind you, as long as they behave themselves. But you come in here and drink too much and then pick a fight with the first person who happens your way. This place was demolished one time by a couple of drunks. I swore it would never happen again."

"I only had one drink," Tom said sarcastically.

"Here, maybe, but how many did you have before you got here? Now do you want to walk out of here on your own two feet or do you wanta be tossed out on your ass?" Harry nodded toward the big bald man beside him.

The bouncer glared at Tom, smiled with his teeth clamped together. He looked like he could crush a man with his thumb.

Tom hesitated, not knowing which way to turn.

"Come on, Champ," Harry said. "Let's dump him on his ass!"

Harry grabbed Tom by one arm. The bouncer took the other one. They shoved him out of the room, down the hall. Harry let go of his arm, ran ahead to open the door while the bouncer literally carried Tom to the exit.

With a forceful kick in the pants and a powerful shove, the bouncer hurled Tom out the back door.

Two shots rang out within a second of each other. The killers had reacted instantly when the door flew open again.

The powerful thrust of the final shove of the bouncer sent Tom's body speeding past the two gunmen. Quicker than they could get their shots off. The twin bullets fried the air behind him.

As his feet finally hit the ground, Tom almost fell over from the forward thrust of his body. His arms shot forward as he tried to break the fall. As his feet propelled him forward, his hands touched the ground. He used his hands to push himself upward again. Another shot whizzed over his head just before he stood up.

He ran straight ahead, out into the darkness of the field behind the saloon. But the two men were in hot pursuit.

The grasses in the field were not more than knee high and there was just enough moon in the sky to cast a pale light across the field. He knew the gunmen could see the outline of his form.

He ran across the open space in a zig-zag pattern, hoping to be a hard target if they shot again.

In the dark, he tripped over a rock, stumbled, fell to the ground. He cursed his luck, scrambled away from the spot on hands and knees. Before he could stand up, another bullet twanged through the air. He felt the hot breeze as it whizzed by his ear, missing him by a scant inch. They had him nailed.

He picked himself up, started running again. He dodged to his right, then cut left. It worked for a few minutes because they couldn't get a bead on him.

He snatched his pistol from his holster on a dead run. He cocked it, turned and fired a round behind him.

His shot didn't hit either of the men who were chasing him, but it slowed them down for a minute as they stopped dead in their tracks, ducked down to avoid getting hit by future shots.

It was enough time for Tom to dash across the open field, seek cover in a stand of aspens. He pulled himself up short next to a thick tree trunk, leaned over and caught his breath. He straightened up, looked back, saw the two shadowy outlines of the gunmen bearing down on him.

He ran deeper into the clump of trees, heard the pounding footsteps coming toward him. A minute later he stopped at the far edge of the trees, heard the crunch of dead leaves as the two men searched for him in the miniature forest of aspens. While the gunmen were in the thick of the trees, he dashed out into the open, cut right and headed for the street.

He reached the back of a building just in time.

A bullet cracked the air just as he rounded the corner of the building. He kept running, reached the street where he turned left and headed toward the Cheyenne Hotel which was still two blocks away.

He covered the first block in record time, but by the time he had reached the corner, the men were shooting at him again as they got to the street and spotted him.

As he ran along the boardwalk with clomping footsteps, he saw something up ahead of him that turned his stomach.

A few buildings up the street, not more than a half a block away, he saw two men dragging a woman into one of the buildings. He knew the struggling girl was being taken into the Lilac House. He would have to pass by the bordello on his way to the Cheyenne Hotel.

His disgust turned to anger when he saw that the girl was Carmen Olay and one of the men was Curtis Dillman. Shit, she hadn't made it! She'd been kidnapped by those filthy bastards!

He raised his pistol, aimed in that direction. But he couldn't get a clear shot. He couldn't risk hitting Carmen.

His stomach churned as he saw the two men drag Carmen on inside the Lilac House.

He ran up to the building a minute later. He hesitated in front of a window, peered through a small slit in the curtain. He was just in time to see a tall, broad-shouldered blonde man rip Carmen's bodice open.

He had to go in there and get her out. Damn, he wished Bolt were there. Together they might stand a chance of getting her away from those filthy men inside.

A shot rang out behind him as the two gunmen closed in on him. He couldn't go in there now. Not with the gunmen so close. He wouldn't make it and he would be of no use to Carmen if he were dead.

He had to get Bolt in a hurry.

He had to get Carmen out of there before the men . . .

He wouldn't let himself think about what they would do to her.

CHAPTER NINE

Inside the Lilac House bordello, Jack Sanders stood in the middle of the large room. He took a slug of whiskey from the glass in his hand, reached down and picked up a bottle from the table beside him. Barely able to focus, he refilled the glass, slopping the strong drink on his shirt and pants. When he spoke, his speech was slurred, his laughter, loud and harsh. But he didn't care. Tonight was his night. His chance to show his power.

The whole room smelled like a brewery. What had been a neat, clean, orderly place earlier that day had now turned into a pig pen with empty bottles littering the floor, cigarette butts stomped out on the polished hardwood floors, ground into the plush lilac-colored carpet in the middle of the room.

Lena Russel had spent a lot of money in furnishing the bordello in her favorite color: light purple. She had taken a lot of care in seeing that everything was decorated with good taste, from the dark purple drapes and sofas, to the lighter shades of lilac in the throw pillows. She had named the bordello the Lilac House because she loved the lilac bushes her father had grown at their home before he died. She had fond memories of those days when she loved to sniff the sweet fragrance of the bushes as she cut the stems of flowers and carried them to the house where she placed them in vases and put them in each room of the house.

The bordello was a shambles now, with cigarette burns in the sofas, the carpet. The furniture was stained with spilled whiskey and beer. Bottles and glasses had been broken and shards of glass were everywhere. Even her favorite hand-painted vase with its floral design of lilacs was broken to smithereens. The paintings of lilac bushes that hung on the walls were not broken, but were tilted at odd angles.

Jack Sanders was taller by a half a foot than any other man in the room. He stood at six foot, five inches, with a large frame, broad shoulders, but not as much muscle as he would have liked. His blonde hair, which was long but usually neatly combed, now hung down on his forehead and was totally disheveled. He had thick fleshy lips, pale blue eyes that were cold as ice. Jack was a lawless man, always had been. He had a reputation that made men walk wide on the street to avoid him. By hook and by crook, and some force, he had gained some political power in Cheyenne, but he wouldn't be satisfied until he had complete power. Even then, he wouldn't be satisfied. His kind never were. Greed and power were the name of his game and he killed anyone who didn't play by his rules.

Surrounded by his drunken sycophants, he appeared to be king of the roost. Uncoordinated by the booze, he swayed back and forth as he boasted about being the new owner of the bordello. He waved his arms as he talked, sloshed whiskey over the glass.

"We gotta lot to shelebrate tonight, my good friends," he said in a loud slurred voice. "I own this fuckin' whorehouse now and that's what we're gonna do . . . fuck them dumb purty girlies all night long . . . until we wear all the hair off their pussies. No charge for the purty whores tonight so fuck 'em all you want. In fact, they should pay us for fuckin' 'em so good."

The men cheered.

"If they give you any lip, just slap 'em down!" shouted Jack. "I own 'em now and they do as I say."

The girls who were not being assaulted at the moment cowered in a corner or struggled to free themselves from the clutches of the rough slovenly men.

"We want 'em to give us lip, Jack!" shouted a man in the group. The other drunks laughed, shouted obscenities.

"Fuck 'em in the ass for all I care," Jack said in his thick-tongued voice. "I'm the boss here. Nobody can touch me now. I'm the most powerful man in Cheyenne and you're my friends. I take care of my friends, don't I?"

The intoxicated men cheered him on. All but one short Irishman who had been tippling most of the day.

"What about that there stranger what took Miss Russel to vote?" called Matthew Malone from a few feet away.

"That bastard named Bolt? What about him?" Jack asked.

"Think he'll come here and try and get this whorehouse back?"

"Ha! You're funny when you drink, Matt," Jack slurred. "Bolt's a coward. I know his kind. Big show he put on at the polls, I hear. He talks big, but he's a godamn coward. A chicken-shit coward. He won't show up. So quit your worryin', Matt."

"But I know what he did to Curt Dillman. I saw him. I was there!"

"Good for you, Matt. Why don't you go get yourself another drink?" Even in his inebriated condition, Jack Sanders understood the implications of Matt's words. He didn't like anyone talking about his men, putting them down like that. It was a sore spot with him anyway. Dillman was supposed to be his best man and he'd let a puny stranger knock him silly in front of half the men of Cheyenne. He'd already talked to Dillman about it, warned him that there'd better not be any more fuck-ups or he'd be through. Dillman had told him he'd take care of Bolt that night, so he should be along shortly with the news of Bolt's demise.

"You ain't gonna let Bolt get away with it, are ya?" Matt Malone persisted. In his drunken state he had a fixation on the subject and wasn't about to drop it.

"Get away with what? You ain't makin' sense."

"With beatin' Curt to a bloody pulp. Don't look too good for you, Jack. Kinda soils your reputation, don't it?"

"Don't worry, Matt, Bolt will be dealt with tomorrow. But tonight it's party time. Why don't you go dump about six inches of turkey neck into one of them whores."

Matt blinked his blurry eyes, then wandered off to get another drink.

Jack held his glass of whiskey high in the air. "Gentlemen," he said, "I'd like to be the first to announce that we have elected a new Mayor today. Now we have total power . . ."

Barry Jewell, who was standing right next to Sanders, reached over and tapped Sanders on the arm.

"Curt. Not now," he whispered.

Sanders turned and looked at Barry with blurry eyes. "I'm just makin' a little announcement." He turned back to the group of men. "Thash not all . . . won't be no more women voting no more . . . we took care of that . . ."

"Curt, please," whispered Barry. He grabbed Jack's arm, tugged on it. Jack staggered against Barry, then regained his balance. "I want to talk to you for a minute." He led Sanders over against the wall where they could be alone.

"I just wanted to tell 'em . . ."

"Curt, the ballots haven't even been counted yet.

You know the official results won't be announced until tomorrow morning."

"But I stuffed the ballot boxes in favor of that law against woman's suffrage."

"Shh. Not so loud."

"You're gonna take care of them phony ballot boxes, ain't ya? Make the switch?"

"Yes, but . . ."

"Then we already know the results. I just wanta make the announcement."

"No. Just let it go for tonight, Jack. Let the announcement come from official sources so it doesn't look fishy. We don't want anyone to know what we're doing."

"Especially your sister, huh?" Sanders grinned and poked Barry in the side with his elbow.

"I don't give a damn about her. You know that. She's a damn troublemaker."

The front door opened just then and Dillman and Barry looked over to see Curt Dillman and Brad Emmons enter the room, dragging a girl in a red dress.

Sanders walked over to them, weaving slightly as he made his way across the room.

"I brought you a present, boss," said Dillman. "She's prime stuff."

Jack recognized Carmen Olay. He'd seen the girl sing at Harry's Poker place before. He'd always wanted to put the meat to her, but she wouldn't give him the time of day.

"Good. She'll add some class to this party. Did you take care of that little matter of Bolt?"

"Couldn't find him, Jack. He's hiding out. I told you he was a damned coward. But I'll get him tomorrow. You can be sure of that."

"You'd better."

"I found his sidekick, though. Seems as if Miss

Carmen here has taken a fancy to Bolt's sidekick. At least they was together tonight, feeling each other up over to Harry's place."

"That right, Carmen?" Sanders asked.

Carmen stood there with her head bowed. She was frightened out of her mind, but she wouldn't let Jack Sanders know that.

"Cat got your tongue, girlie?" Sanders taunted.

She looked up at him and glared.

"So you been friendly with Bolt's partner. What's the bastard's name?"

She continued to stare at Jack, her eyes blazing with hatred.

"I asked you a question, lady! What's his name?" Sanders slapped her hard across the face.

Her head reeled, stung with pain. She bit her bottom lip to keep it from quivering. She fought back the tears that welled up in her eyes.

"Tom Penrod," she said, her voice barely audible.

"Where's Penrod now?" Sanders asked Curt.

"Dead by now," boasted Curt. "Both doors were covered at Harry's. No way he could have stepped outside without being blown away."

Carmen knew different. Tom was still alive. At least he was a couple of minutes ago. Just before the two ruffians dragged her inside the Lilac House, Carmen had gotten a glimpse of Tom running up the street, headed in her direction. She also saw the two gunmen who were chasing him about a block beyond. She had wanted to call out to him, but her mouth was still covered by Emmons' filthy hand. Even if she'd been free to scream, she wouldn't have. She was sure neither of her kidnappers had seen Tom running. Otherwise they would have turned and blown him away. If she had screamed, she would have put him in more danger than he was already in. She prayed that he would make it back to the Cheyenne Hotel alive. She didn't know if he'd seen her and the kidnappers, but if he had, she hoped he'd go for help and come back and rescue her. She wished she could know what was going on out there.

"Maybe he didn't step outside," Sanders said sarcastically. He was irritated that Curt hadn't stayed and finished the job himself instead of leaving it up to the other henchmen. Curt was the best man he had but he was getting damned careless lately.

Sanders didn't like the two strangers, Bolt and Penrod, showing up on election day, either. They were trouble already and they could mess up his plans to take over the control of Cheyenne if they weren't taken out. Maybe Curt was right about Penrod being dead by now. Then he would only have the man named Bolt to worry about. He'd done some checking, found out that Bolt had a reputation for being a hard nut to crack. A fast gun, Bolt didn't back down to anyone, so the informant had said. One of Sanders' men had told him that Bolt owned a string of whorehouses and that he treated whores like ladies and ladies like whores. Well all women were whores as far as Sanders was concerned.

He leered at Carmen Olay, smiled with a lewd curl to his lips. His eyes traveled down her body, saw the large breasts, the bulge of the mound between her legs, the way her tight red dress clung to curves. He'd wanted to jam his cock up inside her pussy for a long time. And he'd do it, too. But not tonight. When he did it to her, it would be in privacy where he could do what he wanted to her. He didn't want a bunch of drunks watching that.

Tonight, he'd turn the pack loose on her, let them fuck her and he could watch. That would serve her right for being friendly to one of the strangers. It would teach her to stick with her own kind.

90

He stepped up to her, grabbed the top of her dress with both hands, ripped the bodice to her waist.

Her bare breasts popped free from the torn dress, exposed for everyone to see.

Carmen gasped. Her hands flew up to her breasts as she tried to cover them.

Sanders pushed her hands away, felt the bare globes as if he were weighing them. He was rough with her and she fought back the tears.

A gunshot was fired outside, someplace close to the bordello. The sound was a faint echo in the din of the room full of drunken men. Nobody paid any attention to it if they heard it. But the sound sent a shiver of fear through Carmen. Tom Penrod was out there someplace nearby and there were two gunmen after him. They could have killed him. She couldn't bear to think of Tom dead. And if he was dead, she would have no chance of getting out of there. No one else knew she was there. Her body trembled when she thought about being raped by any of the men in the room.

Sanders noticed her shiver.

"You ain't cold, are ya?" he laughed. "Well, you're gonna get plumb hot before we're through with ya."

He tore her red dress from her body, ripped it to shreds, left her totally naked before the crowd.

Carmen's eyes were wide with terror as she realized what was about to happen.

"No!" she screamed. "No! Please don't do it to me! Please let me go!"

Jack slapped her again.

"Shut up, you whore!"

He picked her up, heaved her onto the nearby pool table.

"Gentlemen," he announced, "if any of you haven't dipped your wick yet, I'm invitin' you to put the boots to this whore. She was with Penrod earlier, so she must be a whore."

The men crowded around the pool table, started unbuttoning their trousers.

Carmen wanted to die right then. Her fate depended on Bolt and Tom Penrod and she didn't even know if Tom was still alive or if they would come. She knew she was going to be brutally raped. The only thing that was going to delay the act was the fact that the men had already started fighting about who was going to get first crack at her.

"I sure hope Bolt don't show up," mused Curt Dillman when he and Sanders were alone.

"He won't," said Jack, "but I'm taking no chances. I'll station lookouts to watch for that bastard. I'll put two men out front, two more out back, surround the building. He won't get anywhere near this place. He won't even get near either one of the doors."

CHAPTER TEN

Bolt hated to leave Lena and Brenda Loomis alone in his room like that. Sooner or later Curt Dillman or Jack Sanders or one of Sanders' men would track him down, trace him to the Cheyenne Hotel, make him pay for his actions today. He had humiliated Dillman at the polls in front of a large group of townsmen and Dillman would want his revenge. Men like that always did.

Not likely they'd show up tonight, though, since Brenda had said that Sanders was throwing an orgy for his cronies at Lena's bordello. At the expense of the soiled doves who worked for Lena.

Right now he had to figure out how to get those girls out of there before they were hurt. Before they were slapped around and sexually assaulted by the filthy, degenerate drunks who made up Sanders' guest list.

He wished like hell Tom were here to help him. Together, they might be able to get inside the Lilac House and catch Sanders by surprise, get the girls out before Sanders knew what was happening. But he didn't know where to look for Tom. Alone, Bolt knew his chances were slim. Brenda had said that there were more than thirty men at the drunken orgy and seven girls besides herself who were being held prisoner there, forced to submit to the rough and cruel men. Brenda said she had been raped twice, knocked around by the slobs before she managed to escape out a second story window.

Bolt walked down the stairs, past the desk clerk, who

glanced up at him.

"Bad night to be goin' out," said Rodney Sprague. "Cheyenne's a wild town tonight. Full of fightin' drunks. I been hearin' gun shots all evening. Sounds more like the 4th of July. I sure wouldn't go out there among them fools less'n I had to."

"I know," smiled Bolt politely. "Thought I'd write a book about it, do some first-hand research."

"Well, you be careful, ya hear?"

"I will. I'll stay in the background, observe the action from a distance." But Bolt knew he'd be right in the thick of things. By going into the Lilac House, he'd probably be in the most dangerous place in town. He hoped by now the men were good and drunk. That would give him a definite advantage. And if Lena was right about Jack Sanders and his powerful friends, he'd need all the advantage he could get.

Bolt stepped out in the cold night air, pulled his jacket around him to guard against the chill of the breeze that fanned him.

The streets of Cheyenne were much brighter that night because of all the election celebrations. Glowing storm lanterns hung outside almost every building on the main street. Light spilling from the structures added to the brightness of the night, but did nothing to warm it up. The street itself was much more crowded than he thought it would be. Men milled about on the boardwalks, stood in clusters in the street. Laughing and shouting, they guzzled hard liquor from bottles, made fools of themselves. Other men wandered from place to place, trying to find room to drink in the crowded saloons.

Horses and wagons stood idle on both sides of the street while their owners were off someplace drinking the spirits of the raucous night. There'd be a hell of a lot of hangovers in the morning.

Bolt noticed that the street was more littered with debris than it had been earlier that evening. Campaign posters, red and blue streamers and handbills were scattered all over the street and the boardwalks, some of them catching the breeze, sailing through the air for a brief time only to settle down somewhere else. Empty bottles had been dumped wherever men had finished drinking from them.

A minute after Bolt stepped outside the Cheyenne Hotel, he heard loud gunshots off to his left. Bolt looked that way, saw the crowd of men scatter as three men ran down the street, in Bolt's direction. The first men was being chased by the other two men, who were shooting on the run. As the first man got closer, Bolt recognized him.

It was Tom Penrod! Running for his life. With two assassins close on his heels.

Bolt whipped out his pistol, cocked it, ran into the street. As Tom reached him, Bolt fired down the middle of the street. The gunmen stopped in their tracks, returned fire.

The crowd dispersed quickly as some of the men ducked into nearby buildings, others ran down side streets to get away from the fireworks.

As Bolt fired his pistol again, Tom whirled around and cracked off a shot.

The two men following Tom, stopped dead in their tracks, scattered in different directions. One of them ducked into an alley. Across the street, the other gunman ran to the far end of the building on the side street, peeked around the corner of the building at Tom, then ducked his head back.

"Shit, I'm glad to see you," said Tom, panting to catch his breath. He looked behind him, saw that the two men who were chasing him had taken cover.

"What the hell's going on?" Bolt said. He kept his

arm extended, his pistol trained down the street.

"Damn fools are trying to kill me. They kidnapped Carmen!" Out of breath, he hesitated, puffed for air. "They dragged Carmen inside the Lilac House! I saw 'em do it, the bastards! We gotta ... get her out of there ... I just passed there ... looked in the window ... saw 'em tear her dress ..."

"Catch your breath, Tom. I can't understand you."

Tom took a couple of deep breaths, then continued.

"I only got a glimpse inside the Lilac House before those trigger-happy assholes started shooting at me again. But it was long enough to see some tall blonde bastard rip Carmen's dress open. Do you know what they'll do to her?"

"How tall was he?"

"Real tall. Taller than that Dillman feller you took on this afternoon."

"From what Lena told me, that would be the big man himself. Jack Sanders. I was just headed there myself. Seems like Sanders is playing the bigshot tonight, entertaining not only his own men, but those who can do him some good politically. And Lena's girls are providing the entertainment. Now it looks like we got eight girls to rescue."

"Don't know how we're going to do it," Tom said, shaking his head. "There were a couple of men out front near the door. And I saw a man looking out an upstairs window. All with rifles. Maybe we should forget it. Besides, we can't even get to the Lilac House without going by those two fuckin' gunmen."

As if on cue, a shot rang out.

Bolt saw the blossom of orange by the corner of the building where the one man was hiding. He fired a shot just as the man ducked his head back around the corner.

"If we let Sanders beat us now," said Bolt, "he'll have

the last laugh. We're going in after them."

"Hell, man, there's just the two of us. That bastard has fifteen, twenty men siding him. Maybe more."

"Right now, we got just two to worry about." Bolt knew they couldn't stay there. The people had cleared out so that the two gunmen had a free hand. All they had to do was sit tight and wait for Tom and Bolt to make a move. If Bolt and Tom tried to make a run for it, they'd get caught in a deadly crossfire.

"Tom," Bolt asked, "how fast can you shoot that pistol? Can you fan it?"

"Never tried it before."

"Pick that man in the alley. Give him six fast shots. I'm going to rush the other one."

"That's pure suicide."

"Well, we can wait it out here until someone sends in some reinforcements for them. Then, they've got us for sure."

Both of them reloaded their pistols so they'd have a full round.

"Ready?" Bolt asked.

"Yeah."

"Shoot fast. Keep that man in the alley from poking his head out. I won't have time to watch him and get the one around the corner of that building at the same time."

"You got it," Tom assured him.

Tom started firing at the man in the alley. The shots forced the man to keep his head and body out of sight. His gun hand showed once, fired a blind shot then retreated.

Bolt hunched low, ran at the man at the corner of the building on the other side of the street. He waited until he saw the man poke his head around the building, then fired. The man ducked back, fired at Bolt as he did so.

The night erupted with gunfire as all four men

exchanged shots. But Bolt and Tom had the advantage so far. The other two men were shooting blind.

Bullets spanged around Bolt as he ran. He ducked and dodged, kept fairly close to the row of buildings. He couldn't see the man he was gunning for, but he aimed at the last flash of orange, squeezed the trigger.

Bolt heard the man cry out, knew he had gotten him.

The other man stepped out from the alley, returned Tom's fire, then shot at Bolt.

His bullet whizzed by Bolt's head, missing him by a precious inch.

With only two bullets left in his pistol, Bolt swung around, rushed the man in the alley.

The crazed man ran straight for Bolt, fired when he had a good close shot.

Tom took careful aim at the man just before the gunman fired at Bolt. He squeezed the trigger, but he heard only a click. He was out of bullets in his pistol! He couldn't help Bolt now.

Bolt saw the man coming. He jumped to the side just as the man fired. With instant reflexes, Bolt shot at the gunman, dropped him with one shot.

Suddenly, the street was silent and deserted. Deadly quiet.

"Tom, you got a match?" Bolt asked after a minute.

Tom dug down in his pants pocket, drew out a couple of wooden sulphur matches, struck one of them on his trousers. Tom lowered the match as Bolt crouched down and looked at the closest man.

"He's dead," said Bolt after taking one look at the bloody head with one hole between the eyes.

They both moved over to where the other body was sprawled at the side of the street. Tom lit two more matches, held them over the dead man. The man lay in a pool of blood, his pistol still clutched in his hand. Blood stained the front of his shirt, beneath the jacket he wore. The bullet had torn through the flesh, shot straight to the heart. The blood trickling from the corner of his mouth had already stopped flowing, had already begun to dry. His eyes stared vacantly up at the huge expanse of night sky, at eternity.

"Why?" Tom asked in a quiet voice. "Why were they trying to kill me? I did nothing to them."

"You know who they are?" Bolt asked.

"No, but they gotta be Sanders' men. At least they were waitin' for me outside of Harry's Poker place just after Curtis Dillman came in and challenged me to finish the fight that you started. Same group who kidnapped Carmen."

"I imagine Sanders had gunnies staked out at every saloon in town watching for us tonight," Bolt said.

"I reckon so, but it wasn't fair of 'em to steal Carmen like that. She's got nothing to do with any of this."

"Nothing's fair in life, Tom. By the way, who's Carmen?"

"Not what you're thinkin'. She's no whore. Just someone I met."

"She must be a sweet piece of ass to risk getting your balls blown off."

"I couldn't tell you that. I never got that far. But I'd sure as hell like to get her out of the Lilac House and find out for myself."

"She's not the only one. There are seven more gals in there who are being used by brutal, savage men. And we got our work cut out for us."

"How are we gonna do it, Bolt? We're outnumbered about ten to one."

Bolt looked down at the bloody forms of the two bodies in the street then walked a few feet away from them.

"I've got an idea. I hope to hell it works."

Bolt kicked his feet at the posters and handbills that

littered the street. He stooped down, picked up one of the cardboard posters, weighed it in his hand while he was thinking his plan through. He looked up the street, saw that the Lilac House was about a block away. He glanced over at the empty wagons that lined the streets, the restless horses that pulled them.

"What're you gonna do?" Tom asked.

"We're going to make us some fancy signs out of these postboards, similar to the one that Lena wore around her neck. Then we're gonna deliver these bodies to Sanders at the Lilac House."

"You plan on carrying them bloody bodies all the way over to the whorehouse?" Tom said with a trace of sarcasm to his voice.

"Hell, no. We're gonna borrow a wagon."

"Even so, I don't see . . ."

"You will. Now, you happen to have a pencil on you?"

"Matches, yes. Pencils, no."

"Then run inside the hotel and get one from the desk clerk. Get two of them if you can. Then we can each make a sign. Hurry. I want to get out of here before the crowds start to wander back."

It only took Tom a couple of minutes to dash inside and get the pencils from Rodney Sprague. He didn't stop long enough to answer the clerk's questions.

Before they started on the signs, Tom helped Bolt drag the bodies over to the nearest wagon where they left them on the ground.

Bolt carried the two cardboard campaign signs over near a building where the light was better. He handed one to Tom, took a pencil from him. He turned the card over to the blank side, started printing a message on it.

"What do you want me to write?" Tom asked.

"Print 'I PICKED ON A WOMAN' in big letters."

When Bolt was finished with his own sign, he held it

up for Tom to see. It read: 'I PICKED ON THE WRONG MAN.'

Bolt looked around for something to fasten the signs to the bodies, finally found a ball of string in one of the wagons. They hoisted the bodies up into the back of the buckboard. Working quickly, they each tied a sign around a dead man's neck.

Bolt climbed up in the driver's seat. Tom unhitched the horse that pulled the wagon from the hitchrail, then climbed up in the seat beside Bolt.

"I don't see how this is going to work," Tom said as Bolt snapped the reins and the horse began to move. "Seems to me this is going to add fuel to the fire."

"I'm counting on it, Tom. It has to work. It's the only game in town."

CHAPTER ELEVEN

The buckboard was headed in the opposite direction from the Lilac House, which was fine with Bolt. If there were men posted out front, then he'd ride in the back way, use the back entrance to deliver the two dead bodies.

Bolt glanced back up the street one more time. From that distance, he could see that there were quite a few men along the boardwalks on that end of the street. Maybe a dozen or so men in front of the place where the Lilac House was located. But it was too far away to be sure if any of the men were guarding the place or whether they were just men celebrating.

Their pistols reloaded, Bolt and Tom were ready.

Bolt cracked the reins again as the horse and buckboard moved out into the street, headed away from the Lilac House. Bolt turned left at the first side street, then left again when they reached the alley that ran along behind the buildings for several blocks.

The alley was darker than the front of the buildings and Bolt didn't notice the three men in back of the Lilac House until they were almost there.

"Damn," Bolt said, "looks like they've got the back entrance covered too."

The wagon moved slowly in the alley, creaking and groaning as it went.

"What are you going to do now?" Tom asked.

"If they're looking for us, I don't think they'll be expecting us to arrive by buckboard. Just act like we belong here. But when they get a load of these bodies, they're gonna know something's up, so be ready to shoot."

As the buckboard approached the back of the Lilac House, Bolt slipped his pistol from its holster, held it close to his body. Tom's pistol was already out.

He brought the wagon to a halt right in front of the back door. Immediately, the three men who were standing guard came over and stood beside the driver's seat of the buckboard.

"You lookin' fer something?" the closest man asked. He held a rifle in his arm, but it was not aimed at Bolt. The other two men who were standing off to his side also carried rifles, but the barrels were pointed at the ground.

"Just goin' into the Lilac House," Bolt said casually as he slid down from the seat. He let his feet touch the ground, turned to face the large man in front of him. He held his right hand against his leg, the pistol ready to cock. In the darkness, the pistol was not easily visible.

"They're havin' a private party in there," said the guard. "Invited guests only."

"Got a delivery," Bolt said.

"For who?"

"Jack Sanders." His hand moved quickly as he trained his pistol on the guard.

Still up on the seat, Tom scooted across the seat, aimed his pistol on the other two men.

"You ain't . . ." the closest guard started to say.

Bolt brought his pistol up high, clubbed the guard on the top of the head.

The guard gasped, then fell to the ground, completely unconscious.

The other two guards started to raise their rifles, but Tom had them covered.

"You move a muscle and you get your brains blown

out," Tom warned, as he cocked the hammer back. "That goes for both of you."

Bolt turned on the two men, aimed his pistol at them. Tom climbed down from the wagon carefully keeping his pistol trained on the men.

"Drop your weapons," Bolt ordered. "I've got a job for you."

The two guards looked at Tom's pistol, then at Bolt's. They eased their rifles down, let them fall to the ground.

Bolt stepped in, kicked the rifles out of reach.

"Now lift them bodies out of the buckboard," Bolt ordered, "and carry them inside. We're going to deliver them to Sanders."

"Oh, my God!" said one of the guards as he stepped to the back of the wagon and saw the bloody pair on top of the flat buckboard. There was barely enough light in the alley for him to recognize the faces of the dead men. "That's Pete and Whitey!"

"Jesus!" said the second man as he stepped up to view the bodies.

"Pick 'em up. Carry 'em inside," said Bolt.

"You'll never get away with it," said the first guard as he stood his ground, refusing to cooperate with Bolt.

"Just as easy to kill the two of you and deliver your bodies to Sanders along with these," said Bolt, jabbing his pistol in their direction.

Reluctantly, the two guards lifted the heavy bodies from the back of the buckboard. Each of them carried a bloody body in his arms, staggered under the weight.

Bolt walked ahead of them, opened the back door to the Lilac House, then stepped aside to let them go first. The back hall of the bordello was empty, but well lit with lanterns hanging from the walls.

The loud voices of drunken men filtered through to the hallway and the smell of whiskey was stifling. It mingled with the stench of urine that hung around the back door.

Bolt moved around, adjusted the signs around the necks of the dead men so the messages were clearly visible.

One of the guards looked down at the sign on the body he carried. His lips moved when he read, "I PICKED ON A WOMAN." He glanced at the other sign and silently mouthed, "I PICKED ON THE WRONG MAN." He stood still, not wanting to move on inside where his boss would see the signs or the bodies.

Bolt stepped back behind the two guards again, ordered them to proceed down the hall toward the main saloon of the bordello where the voices were coming from.

"Tom, you get that woman of yours out of there fast as you can. I hope I can get the other gals to run for their lives. We can count on surprising Sanders some when we go in there, but after that . . ."

"What are you going to do?" Tom asked.

"Shoot out all the lights I can, try for Sanders."

Bolt jabbed the barrel of his pistol into the guard's back.

"Keep it moving," he ordered as he prodded the two men through the back hall into the main saloon of the whorehouse.

"Hold 'em up high," Bolt warned the guards as they stepped into the room. "I want to be sure Sanders can read those signs."

A woman's scream pierced the air as the four men entered the room. Tom looked over and saw Carmen struggling with a drunken man whose pants were down around his knees. There were cuts and bruises on her naked body and her long dark hair was a mess.

Bolt spotted the tall, blonde man across the room

105

just as Jack Sanders turned his way and saw the dead bodies being carried to the middle of the room.

"What the hell . . ." Sanders yelled as he pushed his way through the crowd, his eyes fixed on the bloody bodies. He pulled his pistol from its holster, pushed men aside as he elbowed his way in the direction of the guards holding the dead men.

"See your girl anyplace?" Bolt whispered to Tom.

"Yeah. That's Carmen over there, fighting with the drunk with the limp pecker hanging out."

"Be ready to grab her. Here comes trouble." He watched Sanders coming, waited until the big man got close enough to read the signs on the dead bodies.

"Sonofabitch!" screamed Sanders, his eyes darting from the signs to the bloody faces. He looked beyond the guards, raised his pistol to shoot when he spotted Bolt.

"Now!" Bolt called to Tom.

Bolt aimed at the nearest lamp that was on a nearby table. He got off a quick shot as Sanders was juggling for a position where he could get a clear shot at Bolt or Tom.

The lantern shattered. Flaming coal oil spewed on the closest spectators as the lamp blew apart.

Confusion erupted in the large room as burning men ran through the crowd. Other people screamed, didn't know which way to run.

Bolt ran to the side a few steps, exploded another lamp with a perfect shot.

Tom shoved the two men in front of him, kicked them forward with a powerful thrust. The guards stumbled forward with their heavy loads, toppled on top of the dead men they were carrying. Tom stepped around them, rushed to get to Carmen.

Other shots rang out in the room as Sanders fired a wild shot and other men in the room drew pistols and started shooting, not really knowing where or who the enemy was.

"All you gals in here, run for your lives!" Bolt shouted. "Get outside fast!" Bolt moved about as pandemonium set in. He shot two more lanterns out which darkened the room considerably. Only one lantern remained burning in the room.

Streaks of flame mapped the darkening room as the men and the glitter gals pushed and shoved each other, trying to reach one of the doors.

Sanders tried to get to Bolt to kill him. He was blocked by the mass of screaming, panicked men and women.

Curt Dillman and Barry Jewell fought their way through the hysterical crowd, came to the aid of their boss, Jack Sanders.

"That's Bolt!" shouted Dillman to Sanders. Dillman took aim, fired at Bolt's head.

But Bolt was a moving target. He wasn't in any one place long enough to get a good shot at him. Dillman's bullet whizzed by him, struck a man behind Bolt. The man screamed out in pain as the bullet crashed into him, settled in his shoulder.

Streams of fire lit the bar. Flames licked at the bottom of the purple drapes, started crawling up their length.

A man rushed out the front door, his shirt on fire. Others panicked, tried to squeeze through the door after him.

The frightened throng pushed against the bar at one end of the room. Under the weight, the counter top collapsed, crushed back against the wall. The shelves behind the bar were jarred loose. Bottles crashed to the floor, shattered from the impact. Bits of sharp glass flew in every direction, cutting those who crushed up against the wall.

Tom reached Carmen among the confusion. He hefted her, carried her toward the back door as fast as he could push his way through the throng of people who were shoving in the opposite direction in a frantic attempt to reach the front door.

Flames spread across the lilac-colored carpet, reached the plush sofa. The sofa became a fire tomb as it sucked up the flames. A man was shoved against the burning sofa. The flames jumped from the sofa to his trousers, quickly leaped to his shirt sleeve. The man screamed as the fire scorched his flesh. He ran for the front door, spreading the fire to others as he waved his arm in an attempt to extinguish the searing flame.

"Get her in the wagon!" Bolt shouted as Tom ran past him carrying the naked Carmen in his arms.

Once Tom got to the back hall, he had a clear shot to the back door.

More shots buzzed the air as Sanders, Dillman and Barry Jewell tried to shoot at Bolt.

Bolt shot out the last lantern, plunging the big room into darkness except for the flames that streaked through the saloon. He turned and followed Tom out the back. A hail of bullets followed him down the back hall, fried the air over his head as he dashed out the door.

He jumped up in the wagon a brief minute after Tom and Carmen had settled on the seat.

Bolt cracked the reins.

The horse raised its head in the air, snorted, then began to move away from the building.

Bolt looked back over his shoulder, saw the angry men spewing out the back door.

The wagon clanked up the alley, picked up speed as the horse gained momentum.

Shots rang out in the dark.

Bolt held his breath, cursed the horse for not going

faster. Behind him, men shouted and swore, fired shots into the night.

At the first side street, Bolt turned the wagon to the right, headed away from the main street because he did not want to drive the wagon in front of the Lilac House in order to get back to the Cheyenne Hotel. He cut right again at the first cross street, rode behind the Lilac House, a full block behind it. From that distance, they could hear the shouting crowd near the bordello. They saw flames lapping at the windows. So far the fire had not spread to the second floor or to the roof, but if it wasn't extinguished soon, the whole place would go up in smoke.

He had seen several of Lena's glitter gals run out the front door when the fire first started. He hoped they all made it. He hoped the men made it too. It was not his intention to kill innocent men.

Two blocks later, Bolt turned right again, headed for the main street. He reined up on the horse just before they reached the corner where they would have to cross the main street again to reach the hotel. The street was fairly bright.

"We walk from here," he said. "No way I'm gonna take this wagon across the street and risk being spotted by some clown."

"By the way, Bolt," said Tom, "this is Carmen Olay."

The frightened, nude girl was huddled in Tom's arms, shivering.

"Pleased to meet you," Bolt said.

"Thanks for the help," she stuttered, her teeth chattering in the cold.

"It wasn't nothing, ma'am." Bolt smiled. "I had business there anyway." He couldn't help but notice her beautiful bare body in the dim light. He slipped his jacket off, handed it to her. "Here, put this on. We're going to make a dash for the hotel. It's just across

109

the street."

Tom helped her put the jacket on and then they all climbed down, abandoned the wagon. As they crossed the street, Bolt looked up the street, saw the glow from the burning Lilac House at the far end of the next block. A crowd had gathered in front of the bordello and had already formed a bucket brigade to put the fire out, getting the water from a large watering trough at the end of the block.

Inside the Cheyenne Hotel, they walked by the desk clerk.

Rodney Sprague's mouth fell open when he saw Carmen's naked body beneath the jacket. He tried to ignore the creamy white breasts that were exposed, but he could not take his eyes off of them.

"There's a building on fire up the street," he finally stammered. "Did you happen to see it?"

"Sorry to hear it," said Bolt as he walked right on by.

"We'd like to help 'em out," Tom explained to the befuddled desk clerk, "but we're plumb tuckered out."

"I can imagine you are," Sprague said sarcastically his eyes still on Carmen's naked body.

The trio went upstairs. Tom took Carmen to his room while Bolt knocked on his own door, called out to Lena that he was back.

Lena opened the door, threw her arms around Bolt.

"Oh, I've been so worried about you. I heard all the shots and I didn't know . . ."

"Lena, the Lilac House is on fire," Bolt said.

"What about the girls? Did they get out?"

"I'm pretty sure they did. I don't think any lives were lost, but I think your bordello is going to burn to the ground."

"I don't care about that," she said. "I can always rebuild. I'd rather have it burn up than let Jack Sanders

110

have it. Do you think he'll find us here?"

"I don't think Sanders is bold enough to storm the hotel. Not yet. He'll be busy trying to keep the Lilac House from burning down. Besides, I don't think he knows where we are."

"But he'll find out, won't he? What about tomorrow?"

"We'll worry about that tomorrow."

He took her in his arms, kissed her passionately.

When he opened his eyes, he saw Brenda Loomis getting up from the sofa. She looked funny in his shirt and baggy trousers which she had slipped over her tattered outfit.

She winked at him, headed for the door.

"If you folks don't mind, I think it's time for me to leave," she said.

"Where are you going?" Bolt asked. "You can't go out on the street tonight."

"Hadn't planned to," she smiled slyly. "Mr. Sprague offered to fix me up with a free room for the night when I came looking for the both of you. Think I'll take him up on his offer."

"Sprague?" Bolt said. "If he offered you a free room, he's gonna expect something in return, the horny bastard."

"I'm counting on it," husked Brenda. "I like the guy. He's always been a pretty decent customer."

Bolt shook his head and laughed. "To each his own, I guess."

"Thanks for the loan of your clothes, Mister Bolt," Brenda said. "I just helped myself. Hope you don't mind. I'll return them in the morning."

"Keep them until you can get your other clothes," Bolt said.

"I'll have some new clothes by morning," she

grinned. "Rodney Sprague will see to that."

"You're wicked, Brenda." Bolt smiled. "You know that?"

"That's what I've been told." And then she was gone.

Lena grabbed Bolt and kissed him, her touch full of promise.

"To each her own," she whispered in his ear as she led him into the bedroom.

CHAPTER TWELVE

After making love to Lena again, Bolt slept restlessly the rest of the night. Fully expecting Curt Dillman or Jack Sanders to break into his room at any moment, he had slept with his ears trained for any strange sounds. He had not allowed himself the comfort of a deep sleep. Finally, with the first light of dawn, he was able to relax and fall sound asleep.

When he woke up, he stretched his arm across the bed, searching for Lena to draw her into his arms. But the bed was empty. With a start, he realized she was gone. He jumped out of bed, slipped into his Levi's. He dashed into the sitting room just as Lena rose from the sofa and came toward him.

"Well, you're awake, sleepy head." She smiled and put the book she had been reading down on the coffee table.

"Jeez, you scared the hell out of me," Bolt said. "I thought you'd been kidnapped."

"No. I just didn't want to wake you up. I know you had a fitful sleep."

"What time is it, anyway?"

"After eleven."

"No wonder I'm so hungry. How long have you been up?"

"About three hours."

"How're you doing?" He walked over to her, put his arm around her, drew her close. She looked somber in her same brown dress, but it was more than that. The sparkle had gone from her big blue eyes.

"I'm all right," she said. "It's just hard to realize that my Lilac House is gone. It's been my whole life for over a year now, since John bought it for me. Maybe it's just as well. I don't know. I guess I'm lucky to be alive and if none of my girls got hurt, then I'm grateful."

"I'm sure they all got out alive and maybe it isn't as bad as we think it is. Maybe the place was just gutted by the fire."

"Even so, it would have to be rebuilt. But maybe that would give me something to do. Everything works out for the best. At least that's what my dear father used to tell me."

"Then keep thinking that. Think of it as a chance to grow. Life is full of blessings in disguise. You'll feel better after we grab some grub. Guess we missed breakfast. Settle for dinner?"

"Sounds good."

Bolt looked down at his trousers, saw the blood stains that he hadn't noticed the night before. Stains from the two dead men he and Tom had lifted into the wagon.

"Let me wash my face, put on some clean clothes and then we'll go downstairs and eat."

When Bolt came back into the room with fresh clothes on, Lena looked up at him sadly.

"After lunch," she said, "I have to go back to my place."

"Why?"

"Because I have to start putting my life back together. I wish I could stay here with you for a week, for the rest of my life, but I know that's impossible. I have to get some prospective and if I stay here, I'd want to spend all the time in bed. There's a lot to be done, I know, and yet I feel like I don't have anything to do. Sounds dumb, I know, but I feel so empty without my work, wicked as it may be."

"Hey, don't talk that way. Your work is just as

important as anything else. And I do understand how you feel."

"Besides," she laughed, "I've got to go home and get out of this dreadful dress. I only wore it yesterday to look more refined and mature when I voted."

"Do you think it's safe to be there by yourself?"

"What can they do to me now? I've already voted. My bordello's gone. I can't see any reason why they'd want me now. I'll be safe, though. I live at Dickens Boarding House a block behind the Lilac House. So I won't be entirely alone. I also have a farm house way up in the foothills, but I'll stay in town for now. The farm belonged to John, the man I was to marry. When he died, I got the farm. I spend a lot of time out there, but with things so unsettled, I'll stay in town for a few days."

"Good idea. Now if we don't get something to eat, I'm going to waste away to a mere shadow." He took her arm and led her out the door.

Downstairs, the desk clerk called to Bolt.

"Somebody was in here looking for you about an hour ago," said Rodney Sprague.

"Oh? Who's that?"

"Didn't leave his name. Said he was a friend of yours."

"Was it Tom Penrod?"

"No. I know Penrod. In fact, Tom and Miss Olay are in the dining room now. This feller was a rough looking one. Tall, muscular, real dirty lookin', you know what I mean? I knew he wasn't a friend of yours right off. I knew I'd seen him before, but it took me a while to place the face. He chums around with that Dillman feller. He's one of Sanders' boys."

"What'd you tell him?" Bolt asked.

"Told him I hadn't seen hide nor hair of you. Figured you didn't want him to know you were here. Told him I didn't even know who you were and that no strangers had checked into the hotel in the last week."

"Thank God," Bolt said. He heaved a big sigh. He didn't like being tracked down like an animal, but it was better to know that someone was looking for you than to have them pay you a surprise visit.

"He also asked if I'd seen Miss Russel and I told him I hadn't."

"Think he believed you?"

"Of course. We all have a right to our privacy and I figured if you wanted Sanders and his boys to know you were here, you'd have told them."

"I owe you," Bolt said. He dug in his pocket, drew out a five-dollar bill, handed it to Sprague.

"No need for that," the clerk said, pushing it back to Bolt. "We all have things about us that we don't want spread around. We all deserve our privacy, don't we?" He looked right at Lena when he said it.

"Yes, Rodney," she said. "We all deserve our privacy. Thanks."

"Well, pay me up for another night, then," Bolt said as he slid the bill back across the counter.

"That I'll do."

Bolt and Lena joined Tom and Carmen Olay in the dining room.

"You through eating already?" Bolt said when he saw their dirty dishes. "I was gonna buy you lunch."

"Sure you were," Tom said. "How come you never get generous unless I've already paid for it?"

"Just lucky I guess."

"Well, the elections didn't go the way you wanted them to," Tom said to Lena. "Good thing you voted yesterday while you had the chance."

Carmen sat forward, looked at Lena. "We just got back from the town hall," she said. "They posted the election results at ten this morning and I wanted to see how the voting went. They passed the law against women's suffrage, so we women are no longer allowed to vote."

"I guess I'm not really surprised," Lena said, "but I'm disappointed. I didn't think Sanders had so many followers. It was his law. I know there were a lot of men who were in favor of women voting, but maybe they had a change of heart. Do you know what the vote was? How many for, how many against?"

"No," said Carmen. "The figures were listed but I was so mad I didn't pay any attention to the tally."

"Maybe I was the only one who voted against that dumb law revoking our right to vote."

"Was Sanders there this morning?" Bolt asked.

"No," said Carmen. "And I didn't see any of his men either, which I thought was odd."

"They probably knew how the vote was going to turn out," said Lena sarcastically. "No need for them to bother going to the town hall to read it on the bulletin board."

Tom got up to leave.

"Did the desk clerk tell you that one of Sanders' boys is looking for us?" Bolt asked him.

"Yair. I'm gonna do some checking around, see if he's been asking for us anywhere else."

"Good idea."

"From what the clerk said," Carmen said, "it sounds like it was Brad Emmons. He and Dillman are the ones who kidnapped me."

"Then we've got a name. Let me know if you find out anything. I'd sure as hell like to keep one step ahead of them."

Tom and Carmen left and Bolt and Lena ordered their meal.

"If you insist on going back to your place," Bolt said when they were finished eating, "I'm going to walk home with you. Then I think I'll do a little checking on my own."

"Thanks. I'll feel better with you beside me. I want to

go by the Lilac House and see how bad the damage is."

She knew before they reached the place where the Lilac House had stood the day before how bad it was. The acrid smell of burned wood still hung in the air.

Her heart sank when she saw it. The only thing left of the Lilac House was a chimney and the rubble of charred wood on the ground. There were a few pieces of blackened metal, but she couldn't even tell what they were. Her furnishings were burned beyond recognition, the paintings of lilac bushes, the beds. Everything had been reduced to smouldering ashes.

"Well, she's gone," Lena said sadly.

"Did you have insurance?"

"Yes. I can rebuild. If I have the strength, the courage."

"You'll do it, Lena. You're strong."

Suddenly, she couldn't stand to look at it anymore. She turned away, walked on up the street, around the corner and toward the boarding house. She walked so fast, Bolt could hardly keep up with her. When they reached the boarding house, she invited him in. She was so stunned by what she had seen that she didn't want to be alone just yet.

Mr. Dickens, the owner of the boarding house, looked up from the newspaper he was reading when he heard the front door open. He saw Lena step into the entry hall.

"Oh, Lena, there was a gentleman asking for you a couple of hours ago."

"I'd hardly call him a gentleman," Mrs. Dickens said as she glanced up from her needlepoint.

"Who was it?" Lena asked, stepping into the living room.

"Don't know him, but Nellie's right. He didn't appear to be no gentleman."

"What'd he look like?" asked Bolt.

"Like an outlaw," offered Nell Dickens, "a dirty outlaw."

"Tall and muscular?" asked Lena.

"Yes," said Nell, "and very rude."

"Emmons again," Bolt said to Lena.

"I told him you weren't here," said Clyde Dickens. "Said I hadn't seen you since yesterday morning. Sorry to hear about all your troubles. Sorry the Lilac House burned down."

"That place went up like a box of matches," said Nell. "From here we had front row seats. We were real worried about you when we saw it burning because we thought you were in there. But we found out later that you weren't there."

"That feller who asked about you," said Dickens, "I think he'll be back. He said he'd check back later to see if you had come home."

"Thanks, Mr. Dickens. If you see him again, tell him you haven't seen me yet."

Lena turned and walked out of the room. Bolt followed her down the hall to her room.

"You can't stay here, Lena," he said when they were inside her room. "It's just too dangerous."

"I know. I'd be scared to death."

"Just get some of your clothes and the things you need and stay with me until we get this thing settled."

"I could go out to the farmhouse and stay. Not many people know I have the ranch. I doubt if Sanders knows about it."

"We're not going to take any chances. You're coming home with me. Now pack what you need and let's get out of here."

"You're taking a chance if you take me back to your room with you," she cooed.

"How's that?"

"A chance that you won't get out of bed for a week."

CHAPTER THIRTEEN

"Maybe I should go out to my ranch and stay," Lena said. "Not many people know about it."

"How many people know that you have a room here at the boarding house?" asked Bolt.

"Not many."

"If they tracked you here, what makes you think they couldn't find your ranch?"

"I guess they could. Oh, that scares me. I've got a lot of money hidden out there under my mattress. What if Sanders' men find it? I'd be finished for sure."

"Kind of a bad place to hide money. That's the first place they'd look. You should put it in the bank."

"I've gotten so I don't trust banks either. I don't know who Sanders has behind him, but I know there are some powerful people involved with him. Bolt, could we ride out to the farm so I can get my money?"

"How much you got there?"

"Over two thousand dollars. Except for the little bit I keep in the bank to pay the business expenses, it's all I've got."

"You got a horse?"

"Yes. I keep him at the livery stable when I'm in town."

"I've got Nick over there, too. Get your things together and we'll ride on out."

Lena quickly changed into the riding breeches she wore when she rode back and forth from the ranch. She put on a yellow blouse with a tie at the collar, a brown jacket that matched her pants. She drew her long dark hair back from her face, tied it in a knot, then tucked it under a floppy wide-brimmed hat. She gathered up a couple of dresses, undergarments and a few personal items and stuffed them into a carpetbag.

Bolt took the bag from her as they walked back to the entry hall.

"Where you going?" Clyde Dickens asked when he saw the carpetbag.

Lena looked into the living room, saw Dickens peering over his newspaper.

"I have some business to take care of," Lena said. "I'll be out of town for a couple of days."

Mrs. Dickens looked up from her needlepoint, gave Bolt a closer going over.

"You two wouldn't be going out to your ranch, would you, Lena?"

"No, Nellie," Lena lied. "If anyone asks for me just tell them you don't know where I am."

"Well, that'll be the truth, at least." Mrs. Dickens' voice had a sarcastic edge to it.

Lena smiled sweetly and walked outside. Bolt closed the door behind them. At the street, they turned right, headed for the livery. Lena looked up at the boarding house, saw Nellie Dickens peeking out the window.

"Nice old couple," Lena said, "but boy are they snoopy. They think I should tell them every place I go. They tend to gossip a bit, so that's why I didn't want them knowing my business."

"But they know about the farm, don't they?"

"Of course."

"Let's hope they don't spill the beans to the wrong folks."

They walked the three blocks to the stables, walked inside the big open doors at the front of the building. The smell of hay and horse flesh was strong inside the building, even though the back doors were open as well. Bolt walked over and patted Nick on the rump, spoke to him in a gentle voice. The horse raised his head, his ears perked up.

"We'll be needing our horses for a while, Cecil," Bolt said to the man at the back of the stables.

Besides owning the livery stable, Cecil Hall was the village blacksmith. He was a hard worker, honest as they come, a family man who loved animals. Bolt often judged a man by the way he treated a horse. Too often, he'd seen men whip their horses with the reins, dig sharp spur rowels into their flanks, push them beyond their limits by running them too hard or too long. But Cecil had impressed Bolt when Bolt first brought Nick to the stables the day before. Cecil had immediately taken Nick into his care by talking gently to him, stroking his long nose, patting him on the shoulders. Fact is, Cecil paid more attention to the horse than he did to Bolt.

"Howdy, Mr. Bolt, Miss Russel." Cecil walked away from the anvil, brushed a lock of dark hair from his forehead. "Sorry to hear about the fire, Lena. Is there anything Dorothy and I can do to help you out?"

"Not yet," Lena said, "but thanks for the offer. It's nice to know I've got friends."

"Hell, I feel like you're one of the family. You and Lilac."

"Lilac?" Bolt said, a quizzical look on his face.

"My horse," smiled Lena.

"What a name to hang on a poor innocent horse," Bolt said.

"I rather like it," said Cecil. "You're still my best customer, Lena."

"Sorry I can't say the same about you." Lena grinned.

"Me too, but Dorothy keeps me on a pretty tight rope." It was something they kidded about every time

Lena came for her horse or brought him back.

"I'll have your horses ready in a minute. Ronnie, come help me saddle up Nick and Lilac."

Ronnie Hall leaned the broom against the wall, walked over to the sawhorses where the saddles were kept. Ronnie, who was fourteen years old, helped his father out at the stable when he wasn't attending school.

A few minutes later, the horses were saddled and ready to go.

"Have a nice ride," Cecil called as Bolt and Lena rode out of the stable.

Bolt waved, then touched his boot heel to Nick's flank. At the first street, Lena turned right and Bolt rode up alongside of her as they headed away from the main part of town.

"Nice folks, the Halls," Bolt said as they rode along the tree-lined dirt road that led to the foothills.

"The best," Lena said. "They've been friends a long time. My father and Cecil were good friends and I've known Ronnie since he was born."

Suddenly Lena pulled up on her reins, brought her horse to a halt.

"Bolt, look! Oh, no! It can't be!"

Bolt saw the smoke then, the gray spiral of smoke that rose up in the sky in the foothills of the mountain range.

"Think it might be your place?" he asked.

"It has to be. My ranch is the only one out there!" She snapped the reins. The horse took off in a gallop.

Bolt came up from behind her, rode right on by. Finally, he got a glimpse of Lena's ranch through the trees. He saw the farm house, the outbuildings scattered around the property. The smoke was spiraling up from one of the outbuildings.

"It's the barn!" Lena called as she caught up to Bolt.

123

"Oh, what happened? Oh, Bolt, quick!"

As Bolt rode closer, he saw the two horses out behind the house, in the clearing between the burning barn and the large rambling farmhouse. A tall man sat one of the horses, held onto the reins of the other horse which had no rider. From that distance, Bolt couldn't make out the man's features, but the rider looked like Curt Dillman.

A minute later, Bolt saw someone dashing from the barn toward the house. The running man had a flaming torch in his hand. With horror, Bolt realized that the man was going to set the house afire.

"You stay here," he told Lena. "Stay under the trees so you can't be seen."

"Bolt, you can't go up there! They'll kill you!"

"You don't want your house burned to the ground, do you? That's what they're aiming to do."

"Forget the house," she cried. "Your life is more important!"

Bolt ignored her warning, rode fast and hard toward the farmhouse.

The tall man on the horse saw Bolt coming.

"Let's get the hell out of here," he called to his partner. He dropped the reins of the second horse, jabbed sharp spurs into the flanks of his own horse. He took off at a rapid pace, headed for the cover of the foothills out back of Lena's place.

Bolt saw his face before the rider turned and rode off. He recognized Curt Dillman.

"Just a minute!" the second man called to Dillman. He leaned down, touched the flaming torch to the corner of Lena's farmhouse just as Bolt rode into the yard.

"Hold it right there!" Bolt called. He saw that the sides of the log house had been splashed with coal oil. The logs glimmered in the sunlight from the path of oil

124

across their surfaces.

Startled, the man dropped the torch to the ground, spun around as he stood up.

Bolt drew his pistol, aimed it at the man.

"Back away from there," Bolt ordered. He started to climb down from his horse when he saw the man's hand go for his holster.

"I wouldn't do that," Bolt warned. "Now get back."

The man took a couple of steps backwards, away from the corner of the building, his hand hovering above his pistol.

Bolt slid down from Nick, started running toward the burning corner of the house as the flames ran along the path of the coal oil. When he got there, he started kicking dirt at the flames. Out of the corner of his eye, he saw the man's hand blur as the man whipped out his pistol.

Bolt whirled around, fired his pistol before the man could get his gun cocked. Bolt's bullet caught the man in the chest.

The outlaw staggered backwards as his lungs exploded inside his chest. Blood spurted from the wound, stained his shirt. He clutched at his chest, fell to the ground. His leg landed right next to the torch. The flames jumped from the torch to the trousers, started burning in both directions, traveling quickly to the man's shoes, up to his knee.

The wounded man tried to scream in pain as the flames seared his flesh. But no sound came out except a gurgling noise. Pink foam bubbled out of the side of his mouth. His pistol had fallen from his hand, clattered to the ground out of his reach.

Bolt dashed over to the man, kicked the torch away from the man's leg, then began stomping at the flames that were burning the outlaw's trousers. He jammed his boot into the man's leg several times, heard the bones crunching. He quickly stomped the fire out, then darted over to the corner of the house that was burning.

Shoving his pistol back in its holster, Bolt scooped up a handful of dirt from the ground, threw it at the flames that licked at the heavy logs of the house. The flames at that spot died out, but the fire was moving rapidly along the path of the coal oil in two directions.

Working quickly, Bolt scooped up more loose dirt, tossed it at the skipping flames. The fire scorched the wood, but couldn't seem to dig into the hard wood of the thick logs. Bolt continued working with great speed, throwing dirt on the flames, until he had extinguished all the fire from the side of the house, the front corner of the building. Smoke curled up from the heavy logs all along the path where the flames had been a minute before.

Bolt heard the wounded man gasp for breath. He walked over and looked down at the man. The man's leg was black, scorched from his knee to his foot, the pantleg burned away. It didn't matter anyway. He was dying from the chest wound.

The man stared up at Bolt with pleading eyes.

"Who put you up to this?" Bolt asked.

"Won't . . . say," the man gasped in a voice that was so soft Bolt could hardly hear it.

"Was this Dillman's idea to get back at me," Bolt asked, "or was someone else in on it, too?"

The man moved his head slowly from side to side.

"You're dying, Mister. Do something decent with the last few minutes of your life. Do something decent for the people of Cheyenne and I'll make sure they know you died a hero. Who's responsible for this?"

"San . . . ders."

"Is he here?"

The man shook his head slowly again.

"Were there any other men out here besides you and

Curt Dillman?"

"No . . . only . . . two of . . . us."

"Why? Why would Sanders want to burn down Lena's house?"

"Sanders said . . . if he . . . couldn't have . . . the whorehouse, Lena . . . to lose . . . everything. San . . . ders said . . . burn . . . her house . . . ruin . . . her . . ." The man's mouth fell open. His eyes glazed over with a vacant stare. His head rolled over on his shoulder. He was dead. At twenty-three.

"Thanks, stranger," Bolt said quietly, then turned away.

Lena had been watching from a distance, under the cover of the trees. When she thought it was safe, she rode on to her house. She glanced down at the dead man.

"That's Brad Emmons," she said sadly. "I knew him when he was a nice young boy. He got in with Sanders' group about a year ago and he changed completely. It's sad, isn't it?"

"Yes, it is."

"He had everything going for him before. He was a talented artist. He could carve a painting out of wood like you never would believe. He sold them at the fairs. Why I'll bet half the people in Cheyenne own one of his wood carvings. How could someone so nice let Sanders influence him, turn him into a bad person?"

"I reckon we'll never know the answers to questions like that," Bolt said.

"What makes a man like Sanders tick? How can a man like that come into a town and corrupt so many people?"

"Greed. A lust for power and money. To men like that, power and money are the same thing." Bolt looked up into the foothills, didn't see a trace of Curt Dillman or his horse.

"Looks like we lost Dillman," Bolt said. "You're lucky this house was made of hard logs. The fire didn't have a chance to really get going. If they'd have had more time, they could have burned it down, though. Too late to save the barn. The corner of this house is still smouldering so I'll have to get some water on it to make sure the fire's out."

"There's a big watering trough out back where John used to water the horses. I keep it full for my own horse. If that's not enough, there's a well out back, too. There are several buckets out there. I'll help you haul the water around."

"No, Lena. It won't take me long to do it. Go on inside and get your money. I want to see if we can find that fuckin' Dillman. He's gotta be out there somewhere in those hills."

"He's probably half way back to town by now," Lena said. "That hill back there gets pretty steep in a hurry, but there are a couple of trails that lead back into town."

"Sooner or later, I'm gonna catch up to that bastard. If he still wants to fight me, I won't be so polite the next time."

"I wonder how they found out about this place," Lena said. She shuddered as a chill crawled up her spine. "No place is safe anymore."

"Not with men like Sanders and Dillman around. But it wouldn't be hard for them to find out about your farm unless you were keeping it a big secret. Men like that buy their information."

Bolt went around to the back of the house, picked up two buckets and dipped them into the trough. He carried them back to the corner of the house that was still smoking. He tossed one bucket at the smoking logs, set it down and dumped the other bucket of water across the thick wood. Just as he started to the back again, he heard Lena scream. He looked up, saw her running out the front door.

"Bolt! Bolt! They've taken my money! They've been in here and torn the place apart!"

Bolt dashed up to the door, followed her inside.

The house was topsy-turvy with furniture knocked over, papers and books scattered every place, drawers pulled out and the contents scattered on the floor. As Bolt followed Lena into the bedroom, he saw that her bed had been torn apart, the mattress pushed aside.

"Dillman's probably got it," Bolt said.

"But nobody knew I had that money there. I never told anyone."

"He probably didn't know what he was looking for. They probably ransacked the place just to see if they could find anything valuable. Most people hide a stash of money or gold somewhere on their property."

"At least the house isn't destroyed."

"We can come back and straighten it up another time, but right now, let's get some more water on the side of the house then get the hell out of here."

They dumped several more buckets of water on the side of the wall, until the logs felt cool to Bolt's touch.

"What are you going to do with Brad Emmons?" Lena asked as she looked over at the dead man.

"Should take him to town and deliver him to Sanders," Bolt said.

"No, I'd rather remember him the way he was when we were kids. I think he should have a decent burial."

"Has he got any kin?"

"Not anymore."

"Tom and I will come out later and take him into town. He'll have his decent burial." Bolt walked over and looked again at Emmons' body. He noticed something he hadn't seen before. A bulge under his shirt at the waistline on one side. Bolt thought it was a hide-away pistol. He lifted the shirt. Tucked into the waistband of Emmons' trousers was a bulging flour sack.

"That's my money!" yelled Lana.

Bolt picked up the sack, handed it to Lena. She opened it and saw that her money was still inside.

"Thanks, Brad, for saving my money," she whispered.

Bolt took her hand and led her away. He was awed by the compassion she felt for her old friend who had just about burned her house to the ground.

After she had put her money in the saddlebags she had brought along to get some extra clothes, Bolt helped her up in the saddle.

He mounted his own horse and they rode away from the farmhouse.

As they rode side-by-side, Lena looked over at Bolt and smiled.

"Looks like you've got a bed partner whether you want it or not."

CHAPTER FOURTEEN

By the time they got back to the stables, it was late afternoon. Lena told Cecil Hall about Brad Emmons, about the plans to bring his body back to town for a proper burial.

"Sorry to hear that," said Cecil. "I always liked Brad until he got mixed up with Jack Sanders."

"So I'll be needing to keep my horse with me," said Bolt. "I'll get my friend to ride out there with me and bring the body back."

"Hell, let the undertaker ride out and get the body," said Cecil. "He can handle it easier'n you can because he's got the wagon."

"I don't know why I didn't think of that," said Lena. "It'll save you a trip out there, Bolt."

"That would help," said Bolt. "Tell you the truth, I wasn't really looking forward to another trip out there today."

"Sure, Joe's a good old boy," said Cecil. "Just stop by his place and tell him where to go. He'll take care of everything."

"Good. I guess I'll leave you here after all, Nick," Bolt said. He patted his horse on the rump. "Be a good boy for Mr. Hall."

Cecil took the reins from Bolt, led Nick over to a stall where he began to remove the saddle.

"Your horse is sure in fine condition," Cecil said. "His muscles are well-toned and he's sturdy as an ox. Look at his coat, how it shines. I can tell you take good care of him."

"Yeah, he and I are pretty good friends."

"You should see what shape some of the horses are in when the owners drop them off here. Mangey hides, either skinny with their ribs showin' or bloated bellies from improper food. It's a damn pitiful shame the way some folks treat their animals."

"Yeah, I've seen men literally drive their horses to death by pushing them beyond their limit."

Lena opened the saddlebag on her horse, removed the cloth flour sack and handed it to Bolt. He stuck it in the inside pocket of his jacket.

"You can keep my saddlebags here, Cecil," said Lena. "I thought I'd need them to bring back some of my clothes but after all the trouble, I lost interest."

"Can't say as I blame you. Well, you folks have a pleasant evening. I reckon nothing else can go wrong."

"Don't count on it," Bolt said.

Bolt and Lena left the stables, walked back to the main street, headed in the direction of the Cheyenne Hotel.

Lena's stomach churned when she saw the burned remains of the Lilac House again. They walked along the boardwalk on the opposite side of the street from the burned building. They stopped in front of the undertaker's office.

A wooden sign in front of the building creaked on rusty hinges as the breeze caught. Painted in neat white letters was the legend: JOE MORTON, UNDERTAKER. Under that, in smaller letters were the words: COFFIN MAKER.

They walked into the building, heard the pounding of a hammer coming from a large room at the back of the structure.

Bolt looked around the small waiting room, saw the plush sofa, three overstuffed chairs, a big desk covered with paper work, bookshelves, a filing cabinet. A brass

132

bell rested on one corner of the desk with a sign that read: "Ring for Service." Bolt picked it up, gave it a hefty shake.

A minute later, Joe Morton walked into his office, slipping a black jacket over his white shirt.

"Hello, Lena. I was sure sorry to see your place burn down last night."

"Thanks, Joe."

"What brings you here?" Joe Morton was talking to Lena, but he eyed Bolt suspiciously.

Bolt was stunned by Joe's appearance. He was tall and terribly thin, almost cadaverous. Even his skin was pale and gaunt. His dark eyes were set back too far in their sockets. Bolt was sure that Morton looked more dead than some of the corpses he worked on.

Lena introduced the two men, then explained to Joe about Brad Emmons. "I'll pay for his burial," she said.

"It's twenty dollars. Five bucks extra if you want a coffin."

"Yes, I do."

"Will there be a funeral service?"

"No. He hasn't got any kin and not many friends anymore. Just bury him in the Shady Lane cemetery at the edge of town."

Bolt paid the undertaker from his own money, rather than taking it from Lena's sack. He felt partially responsible for the youth's death, although if he hadn't shot Emmons, the man would have killed him.

They left Morton's office, went directly to the hotel. When they got to Bolt's room, Bolt gave Lena her money. She tried to pay him for Emmons' burial but he refused her money. She put the flour sack inside the carpetbag she had brought from the boarding house, took her dresses out and hung them on hangers in the closet.

"I've got to check with Tom," Bolt said. "Are you

getting hungry?"

"Yes, but I can't go to dinner in my riding breeches. Do I have time to change?"

"No hurry. I'll go talk to Tom while you're getting dressed."

Bolt walked to the door. Just as he reached for the door knob, there was a loud knock on the door. Bolt froze, listened.

"Who is it?"

"Rodney Sprague. The desk clerk. I've got a message for you."

Bolt opened the door, saw Sprague standing in the hall wringing his hands.

"What is it, Rodney?"

"It's your horse, Mister Bolt. Your horse is real sick and it might be dying. You're to go to the livery stables right away."

"Nick? It couldn't be. I was riding him this afternoon. I just left him at the stable less than an hour ago. He was fine then."

"That was the message I got," Rodney said almost apologetically.

"Who delivered the message? Cecil Hall?"

"No."

"His son, Ronnie?"

"No. Some feller I never saw before. Must have been the new man he hired to help him with the blacksmithing. He's been talking about getting another man in there but I didn't know he'd hired him."

"I didn't see anyone else in there when I was there." Something was fishy, but Bolt didn't know what it was. He didn't see how Nick could become so sick in such a short time. Even Hall had commented on what good condition Nick was in. It didn't make sense unless . . . unless Curt Dillman had seen the horse Bolt was riding out at the ranch. It was possible that Dillman had seen

Nick and then waited for Bolt to return. Dillman could have slipped into the stable and poisoned the horse without too much effort. Or maybe Nick wasn't sick at all. Maybe the messenger was one of Sanders' boys. Perhaps it was a trap to lure Bolt to the stable. He didn't know what to do, but he had to get over there right away.

"Do you know where I can borrow a horse?" Bolt asked.

"Use one of mine," Rodney said. "I keep four of them fenced up out back of the hotel. None of them are saddled up, but you're welcome to use one of them."

"Thanks. Would you do me a favor? Do you know if Tom Penrod's in his room?"

"Yes. He came in about an hour ago."

"Go tell him to get over to the stable as soon as possible. I just might need his help."

"Will do."

Bolt took the steps two at a time, dashed across the lobby of the hotel. Just before he reached the door, a well-dressed woman stepped in front of him, blocking his way.

"Mister Bolt," she said, "I would like a word with you."

Startled, Bolt looked at her. She wore a dark blue dress with a high-button collar which made her look much older than her years. She had big brown eyes but they were partially hidden by the glasses she wore. Her light sandy hair was tied back in a bun, covered by a hat that matched her dress. She carried a small carpetbag at her side. Bolt could see that underneath the facade of properness, she was a real beauty—if she only knew how to dress.

"Not now, ma'am. I'm in a hurry." Bolt tried to step around her, but she moved around, continued to stand in front of him.

"My name is Claire Jewell and I'm a schoolteacher." Her voice was low, husky as she spoke.

"I don't have time to talk right now, Miss Jewell," Bolt said impatiently. Again he tried to side-step her, but she was persistent.

"I saw what you did to Curt Dillman yesterday afternoon and I think you're a gentleman for having seen to it that even a lowly woman like Lena Russel got to vote. But, there are irregularities in the ballots and the election authorities refuse to let me and my committee examine the ballot boxes."

"That's a matter for the law," Bolt told her.

"The law won't help me. They just ignore me. I need a man, an honest man, to press for a recount. I'm sure you can understand that."

"Later," he said as he brushed her aside.

She quickly dug into her carpetbag, drew out a small card with her name and address on it. She pressed it into Bolt's hand.

"Tonight," she told him. "Tomorrow will be too late. I only have until tomorrow morning to challenge the results of the election as they were posted this morning. I'll be waiting for you." She turned and walked out the front door.

Before Bolt could go out the door, he heard his name called.

"Bolt! Hold up. I'll go with you." Tom Penrod ran up to Bolt. "Sprague told me to go out the back door to get to his horses. It's quicker."

The two men ran for the back door, rounded up two of the unsaddled horses in the fence, and climbed atop them.

"I think it's an ambush, Tom."

"You mean Nick isn't sick?"

"Don't know. If he is, he's been poisoned in the last half hour. But I'm more inclined to think that

136

someone's waitin' for me to show. I'm riding in easy. Be ready to shoot and watch your step."

"Bolt, I swear I don't know how you get yourself into these fuckin' messes."

"It ain't easy." He grinned as they took off at a rapid clip.

Bolt was taking no chances. Instead of riding up the main street and cutting right to the stable, he took the alley that ran behind the buildings of the main street. The one that ran between Lena's burned bordello and the boarding house where she stayed when she was in town.

He was worried about Nick.

But his gut feeling told him that he was walking right smack into a trap.

CHAPTER FIFTEEN

As they rounded the corner, with the stable still a half a block away, Bolt held his hand in the air. A signal for Tom to haul in on the reins.

Bolt brought the horse he was riding to a halt in front of the Cheyenne Freight Office, one of the buildings along the side street. Tom pulled up beside him.

"We're walking the rest of the way," said Bolt as he slid down from the bare back of the horse. Riding the strange horse made him appreciate Nick even more. Nick was able to respond to Bolt's slightest movement as if the horse could read his mind.

"Good idea," Tom said as he climbed down from the other horse.

The two men tied the horses to the hitchrail in front of the freight office, walked across the street to the side where the stable was located. Bolt kept a careful eye on the stable building as they walked toward it, but he saw no sign of activity outside.

When they reached the corner of the building, Bolt stopped and listened. It was quiet, too quiet inside. No pounding sounds at the anvil like he had heard before. No voices. No clanking metal sounds or rattling of buckets. Only the soft scuffle noises of horses moving about on the straw in their stalls. That bothered Bolt. If Nick were sick, surely Cecil Hall would be inside tending to the horse. And Cecil always gentled the horses by talking to them.

The sun had set a few minutes earlier and it was that time of twilight when it was still light outside, but when anterns were lit inside houses with the approaching darkness. It was also supper time for a good many people as men stopped working outside and went home for their evening meal. That could account for the stables being empty except for the horses, if Cecil had stopped working to eat. But Bolt knew that with Cecil's love for animals, he would never leave the side of a sick animal to satisfy his own needs. Not unless the crisis had passed.

"I'm going in the front way," Bolt whispered to Tom. "You go around and cover the back door."

Tom snuck along the side of the building, being as quiet as possible. When Bolt saw him reach the back and round the corner, Bolt moved toward the open double doors of the front of the stable. He paused, listening again, then stepped quickly inside the barn. Knowing that his silhouette in the door frame was a perfect target with the light of dusk behind him, Bolt moved to his left, stood next to the wall while his eyes adjusted to the dim light inside the stable.

He saw Tom's silhouette move into the wide door frame at the back, then quickly disappear into the darkness as Tom moved inside. Bolt scanned the room with his eyes, saw Nick in the fourth stall on the left. Nick was standing on all fours and his head and long neck showed above the slats of the stall.

There were horses in every stall on that side of the room. Eight of them. There were eight stalls along the opposite wall, but only six of them were occupied. Horses in the first two stalls, the third one empty, Lena's horse in the fourth slot, the next one empty and three rental horses in the last three stalls at the back. Behind the last stall on the right side was where Cecil had set up his blacksmith shop. Tom's horse was in the stall next to Nick, on the side closest to Bolt.

Bolt glanced again at Nick. The horse didn't appear

to be sick, but in the dim light and from that distance he could only tell that the horse was well enough to be on his feet.

Bolt took a step in Nick's direction. Straw crunched beneath his boots. The sound magnified and echoed in Bolt's ears. He stopped, listened for any other sounds. He looked to his left, studied the dark shadowy figures near the front wall. He made out the eerie forms of saddles resting on sawhorses, the ghostly hulks of saddlebags hanging above them, held in midair by nails fastened to the wall. A broom and shovel leaned into the corner like a pair of dark ominous watch dogs.

Satisfied that he had identified each and every threatening shadow and that on one was lurking in the dark corner, he looked to his right, beyond the open doorway. He went through the same process of scrutinizing every billowy shadow that could be a human being. The saddles sitting on sawhorse perches looked like a row of crouching gunmen in the darkness. The tack, hanging from the wall, resembled foreboding weapons.

A dark form in the middle of the area between the front wall and the first stall on the right caught his eye. It looked more like a large man hunching down than anything he'd seen. When his eyes fell on it, his heart skipped a beat. He held his breath, stood perfectly still as he watched it carefully. The dim light from outside played tricks on Bolt's eyes. He swore he saw the dark form move.

He squinted his eyes, focused on the shape that looked exactly like a large crouching man. Starting at the floor level and working up he analyzed each curve and angle of the dark mass. When he realized what it was, he breathed a sigh of relief, almost laughed out loud at himself for being so frightened. The object that had appeared so human-like was nothing more than a big round barrel of grain in the middle of the floor. What made it look so real was the bucket sitting on top of it, the man's hat set on top of the bucket and a shirt or jacket that had been thrown across the top of the barrel next to the bucket. An axe handle or some long tool, also placed on the barrel top, had looked like a rifle barrel at first. It was obvious, now that he knew what the objects were, that the top surface of the grain barrel had become a catch-all for things that Cecil or Ronnie had to set down. He looked at it again and smiled. Even now, though, the form appeared to move.

Bolt wondered where else a man could hide in the big roomy barn. Almost anyplace, he reckoned, but Tom was in a position to check out the back of the barn. That left two likely places. The two empty stalls on the right side of the stable. The stalls on either side of Lena's horse. Both of them were ideally located if a man wanted to hide and shoot at someone who might walk to Nick's stall, which was directly across from Lena's horse.

Bolt took a couple more steps toward Nick's stall. He cursed the sound of his boots crunching on the straw. Keeping his eyes alert for any sudden movement, he made his way across the floor to the first stall on his left. He eased across the open space, the horse behind him, reached the slats that separated the first two stalls.

He was just about to take another step when the closest horse whinnied. The loud shrill cry set Bolt's heart pounding again. His foot stopped in midair and he didn't move again until he recovered his composure.

He crossed in front of the next two stalls with little effort because all of the horses, nervous from the first one's cry, moved about in their stalls.

He was now at the corner of Nick's stall.

Getting a whiff of Bolt's scent, Nick threw his head in

141

the air, lowered it, then tossed it high again and whinnied. It was something the horse did every time Bolt was away from him for any length of time and then returned. A welcoming gesture. Only right now, Bolt didn't appreciate it like he usually did.

He reached behind him, patted Nick on the rump. The horse scuffled his hooves through the straw, tried to turn around. Bolt patted him again.

Straining his eyes, Bolt tried to peer into the two empty stalls across the way. The big room was growing darker by the minute. He could see the front parts of the stalls, but the back area of each stall fell into darkness.

Another sound caught Bolt's attention. He stopped where he was, listened with careful eyes. Footsteps! Someone was coming! Soft footsteps crunching the ground out back of the stable. Approaching the back door.

Bolt's hand moved over to his side, hovered over his pistol. He watched Tom's outline at the back of the room, saw his friend draw his pistol, aim it toward the door.

The footsteps got closer.

Bolt tensed.

Tom stood motionless, waiting.

And then the silhouette appeared in the frame of the open back doors.

It was a woman! Short and wearing a long dress!

Bolt watched her carefully as she entered the room, turned immediately to her left—away from Tom. She hadn't seen Tom, he was sure, because Tom was in the shadows.

Tom watched the woman, too. He had come very close to shooting her when she stepped inside. But he had learned a long time ago not to shoot unless he was absolutely certain who he was shooting at.

Just beyond the door frame, the woman turned again, faced the back wall, her back to Bolt. There was just enough dusk light left outside to show her outline. If she had been any farther away from the door, she would have been lost in the darkness.

Bolt saw her arms reach up high. A minute later he heard the clatter of a lantern, a rubbing sound as her fingers searched a table for matches. The scratch-pop sound as she struck the match on the rough wall. She touched the flame of the match to the lantern wick, adjusted the wick when the fire caught. She replaced the glass chimney, stood on her tiptoes to hang it back up on the high nail.

The light from the lantern cast a soft glow across the big barn. Immediately, Bolt's eyes searched the two empty stalls across the room. From his position he could see the entire area of both stalls. And they were, indeed, both empty. Something funny was going on and Bolt couldn't figure out what it was. Another thought struck him. Maybe there was nobody here waiting to ambush him. Maybe he had been lured away from the hotel so Sanders and his men could get to Lena.

The woman turned around. When she saw Tom standing across from her, his pistol aimed in her direction, she gasped, jumped a foot.

Tom quickly shoved his pistol back in its holster.

"Sorry, Mrs. Hall," Tom said. "Didn't mean to frighten you."

She clutched at her chest with small fists as if to quiet her pounding heart.

"Oh, mercy," she said. "You scared me half out of my wits. I just came out to light the lantern. I had no idea anyone was out here."

Just then she caught a glimpse of Bolt out of the corner of her eye. She gasped again, caught her breath,

143

let it out slowly when she recognized Bolt.

"Evening, Mrs. Hall," Bolt said.

"Oh, Bolt, I'm glad it's you two and not some horse thief out here. I don't know what I'd have done." She laughed, a trace of hysteria in her voice. "I guess I'm a little spooked tonight with Cecil gone."

"You're not the only one," Bolt laughed. "Cecil's gone, you say?"

"Yes. He had to deliver two of our horses to some folks who live way out of town. Ronnie went with him so I told Cecil I'd walk over from the house and light the lantern. Were you looking for him?"

"Sort of," Bolt said. "I got a message that my horse was very sick, that he might be dying." Bolt glanced around at Nick. The horse looked to be in perfect health. "I thought Cecil would be here tending to him."

"Hmmm, that's odd," she said, stepping a few feet closer to Bolt. "Cecil never said a word about it. I'm sure he would have told me if any of the horses were sick. And I'm quite certain he wouldn't have left if there was a sick horse. No matter who wanted a horse delivered."

"That's what I figured. Do you know who ordered the horses that he's delivering?"

"Some fellow named Smith, is all I know. I was out here talking to Cecil, bringing him a cup of coffee, when the stranger came in. You and Lena had just left a few minutes before that. Cecil told me you was here and we were talking about her bad luck when the Smith fellow came in. Said he was new in town, that he was purchasing some farm land outside of town. Said he needed two horses right away. I went back to the house while they were discussing business. Cecil came in a few minutes later and said he was leaving and that I should light a lantern in the stable come dark."

"Did the stranger pay for the horses?"

"No. Cecil said the fellow would pay him when he delivered the horses."

Sounded to Bolt like Hall had been sent on a wild goose chase, but he wouldn't say anything to Mrs. Hall about his suspicions. No use in worrying her any more than she was already.

"Well, I'm going to check my horse out while I'm here," Bolt said. "When Cecil gets back, tell him I was here. Maybe he can help unravel all this."

Dorothy Hall plunked her hand on her hip, wrinkled her brow in puzzlement.

"Mighty odd about that message you got," she said after a minute. "About your horse being sick. It's really got me puzzled. Who told you about your horse?"

"The desk clerk at the hotel. Rodney Sprague."

"Suppose he was playing a little prank on you?"

"Somebody was," Bolt said sarcastically. "Did your husband hire a new man to help him out?"

"Mercy no. Oh, he's been talking about it for a long time now, but he hasn't been able to find a good worker yet. They're hard to come by these days, you know. Times aren't like they used to be when a man wasn't afraid to put in a good day's work for a good day's wages. Why do you ask?"

"The desk clerk said he figured it was Cecil's new hand who came in and told him to give me the message about my horse being sick and that I should come right away. Sprague said he'd never seen the man before."

"That's even more puzzling." She shook her head. "Somebody's got a weird sense of humor to pull a stunt like that on you. Myself, I don't think it's very funny."

"I don't either." There was a cold, bitter edge to Bolt's words.

In the stall right next to Nick's, beyond where Bolt was standing, Curtis Dillman cursed his luck.

Up until a few minutes ago, everything had been going like clockwork. Just the way he and Jack Sanders had planned it. The new man Sanders had hired had worked out real well. He had said his name was Gripper, but nobody knew if that was his first name or last. Gripper had done his job at the stable, convincing Hall to deliver those two horses to a farm that didn't exist, and he did it without paying up front. Hall would be madder'n hell when he discovered that there was no such farm or even a house out that way.

And Gripper had played it to the hilt when he gave the desk clerk the message to relay to Bolt. Nobody had even suspected that it was a trick to get Bolt to the stable alone.

Of course he and Sanders hadn't counted on that Penrod fellow coming along with Bolt, but even that didn't bother Dillman. He could take both of them out as easy as one. He had known Penrod was standing by the back door. He'd seen him come in, just the same as he saw Bolt's silhouette when he came through the front door.

The timing was perfect. Bolt had arrived just as it was turning dark. Dillman's eyes had already adjusted to the darkness of the room, so he figured he had a big advantage. He could see both men, keep track of them and yet there was no way they could spot him inside that stall.

He knew things were going right for him when Bolt started to make his way over to that dumb horse of his. That was what he was waiting for. For Bolt to walk into his horse's stall. That's when he planned to shoot Bolt's brains out. Bolt wouldn't even know what hit him.

But Hall's woman had come in at the wrong time, just seconds before Bolt would have stepped into the stall. And she'd lit that damn lantern. He hadn't counted on that. The whole damned barn was lit up now so he didn't have the same advantage as he had before.

He wished the woman would shut up and go back to her house. His legs were beginning to cramp. He'd been in a crouching position too long now. Longer than he'd planned. The horse in the stall where he was hiding kept bumping into him and he was afraid the damned animal was going to kick him in the head. The stench of horse piss and wet straw was overpowering inside the stall and he was beginning to feel sick to his stomach.

He knew Bolt was suspicious now that he was talking to the woman, but Dillman knew his plan could still work. It had to work. He couldn't face Sanders if he bungled any more jobs.

If the woman would leave, Bolt would go in the stall with his horse. It would still be easy to kill the bastard because Bolt didn't know he was there. And if Penrod didn't run out the back door, Dillman would turn and shoot him before he knew what was happening.

Yes. His plan would work. He might even get two for the price of one.

CHAPTER SIXTEEN

Mrs. Hall turned to leave.

"By the way," she said, "I baked a cake for Lena. To cheer her up. Would you mind taking it to her, Mister Bolt?"

"Be happy to. She could use some cheering up."

"When you're through here, stop by my house next door and I'll have it ready for you."

"Tom, why don't you walk over with Mrs. Hall and get the cake while I check Nick. By the time you get back I'll be ready to go."

"Sure," said Tom. "I reckon I can carry a cake this far without dropping it."

"You'd better," laughed Mrs. Hall. "It's her favorite, chocolate applesauce. She might even share it with you."

As Tom and Mrs. Hall went out the open back door, Bolt stepped into the stall with his horse. He patted Nick high on the rump.

"How you doin', old boy? Feelin' pretty frisky?"

The horse threw his head in the air, whinnied, as if to answer Bolt's question.

Bolt walked along Nick's side, the side that was closest to the front door. He ran his hand along Nick's flanks, then leaned down and felt each long leg with both hands to see if he could feel any quivering muscles that would indicate that the horse was weak.

As he walked around in front of his horse, Nick nudged Bolt's shoulder with his nose.

"Atta boy," Bolt said, scratching the animal under

the chin, rubbing the long nose. "You sure don't look sick to me." He turned the horse's head toward the light, checked his eyes. The horse seemed to be in perfect condition.

As Bolt moved around to the other side of the horse, the side nearer the back door, he got a slight whiff of a familiar scent. It smelled like stale hair tonic mingled with horse flesh. But the scent was so vague he paid little attention to it.

He stood at Nick's side, stroking the horse's hide, feeling for feverish spots or broken bones.

The only light in the roomy stable came from the back of the room. The five-foot-high wooden divider between Nick's stall and the one next to it threw a shadow across the straw-covered ground on that side of the stall. The shadow extended to the tops of Nick's long legs.

With the light to his back, Bolt's own shadow fell across the horse's back. When he leaned down to check Nick's other legs, his shadow disappeared from the animal's back. With the good light now on Nick's side, Bolt glanced back up, saw that Nick's hide was shiny, healthy looking.

As he reached over to check Nick's front leg, Bolt sensed that it was growing darker in the barn. For a moment he wondered if the lantern was getting low on fuel, if the flame was dying out. Then he noticed that the shadow inside the stall was expanding, spreading across the floor of the stall.

He glanced up at Nick, saw the shadow slowly growing up on the animal's side. His heart skipped a beat. A chill ran up his spine. The hackles rose on the back of his neck as he realized that there was someone right behind him, in the next stall.

Without moving, he watched the shadow move across Nick's back. He saw the silhouette of an arm float across the horse's shoulder, a hand, the shadow of a pistol gripped in that hand.

Still crouched down, he reached up and patted Nick on the side with his left hand. "Good boy, Nick," he said to cover the sound of his other hand moving to his holster, drawing his pistol. His thumb rested on the hammer, his finger eased into the trigger. He eased his back against the wall of the stall, pointed his gun upward.

He watched the shadow on Nick's shoulder, saw the shadow of the other pistol point down. He had to make his move.

Just as he heard the ominous click of the other pistol being cocked, he ducked to his left, looked up and saw Curt Dillman staring down at him over the stall divider. His eyes focused on the dark hole of Dillman's pistol barrel. He saw the long dark hole follow him as he ducked to the left, as the outlaw adjusted his angle.

Without hesitation, moved again, thumbed down on the hammer and squeezed the trigger in a smooth, easy motion.

Dillman's head snapped back as he took the bullet under the chin. The boom of the exploding gunshot blotted out Dillman's scream an instant later. As Dillman's hands started to reach for his wounded neck, his grip loosened on the pistol. The pistol clattered to the ground inside the stall.

Dillman's hands never reached his burning neck. As they got chest-high, the bullet sped to his brain, exploded, took the back of his head with it when it exited. Dillman stumbled backwards, bumped against the horse in the stall. The horse neighed, shied away from the commotion. Dillman's body slid down the horse's front legs, crumpled to the damp straw floor.

Bolt dashed around the five-foot wall that separated the two stalls. His pistol was already cocked, ready to shoot again. But there was no need. Dillman was dead, pieces of brain matter spattered on the horse, on the wall, a pool of blood under his head.

Bolt looked at the man in disgust. He saw a piece of paper sticking out of the dead man's shirt pocket. As he leaned over to take the note out of his pocket, he got a whiff of the same scent he had smelled a few minutes before. The smell of stale hair tonic. He shuddered when he thought how close he'd come to death. He had been careless and it almost cost him his life. He should have paid more attention to the faint odor when he first smelled it.

He opened the small piece of paper, saw a sketch of the inside of the stable. Two of the stalls in the sketch were specifically marked. One of them had the notation, "Bolt's Horse." The stall next to it simply had a big X in it. At the edge of the paper was a note: "Plan for sunset. Dark inside."

Someone had gone to a lot of trouble to set him up so they could kill him in cold blood. It wasn't over yet, he knew, not as long as Jack Sanders was still around. Not as long as Sanders lusted for power.

Tom dashed through the back door of the barn, pistol drawn. He saw Bolt's head above the stalls.

"What the hell's going on?" he called.

"Damn near got my head blown off by this sneaky bastard."

Tom came over to the open end of the stall, looked down at Dillman's body.

"Looks like his fighting days are over," Tom said as he shook his head.

"Too bad their scheme didn't work for them," Bolt said sarcastically as he handed Tom the note with the sketches. "They had it all mapped out."

Tom looked at the sketch.

"Shit, these guys take it serious, don't they," he said.

"They're out for blood."

"Don't worry, they'll try again."

"It's a wonder the guy didn't blow you away when you were walking across the barn. Hell, you sounded like a herd of elephants plowing through that straw. I could tell exactly where you were, even when I couldn't see you." Tom handed the note back to Bolt.

"Damn right. I was giving the bastard an easy shot. No, the man had a plan and evidently he was going to stick to it, come hell or high water. I've known a lot of assholes like that. Able to follow simple instructions but without brain one when it comes to thinking up an original idea."

"What do we do now?"

"Drag this body out front for one thing. Cover him up, leave him there until the undertaker can take care of it."

Bolt stuffed the note in his pocket. When he drew his hand out, a small white card fell to the ground. He picked it up, glanced at it, then remembered his hurried conversation with Miss Jewell in the hotel lobby. He guessed he could take the time to go see her now, see what was on her mind.

After Bolt and Tom had dragged the body out the front door, thrown a horse blanket on top of it, they went back inside the barn.

"I've got to go back over to Mrs. Hall's and get that cake for Lena," Tom said. "When I heard the shot, I left it on the table."

"Tom, I got a couple of favors to ask you."

"How come I smell trouble every time you ask a favor of me?"

"You'll love it this time. I'm just asking you to take two beautiful women out to dinner."

"Who's that?" Tom looked at his friend suspiciously.

"Lena and Carmen. I promised Lena I'd take her out

152

to eat, but I've got something I've got to take care of. I'll take my own horse."

"Who's buying?"

"You are," Bolt laughed. "After all, you'll be the one to have the pleasure of their company."

"It figures. What about the horse you borrowed from Sprague?"

"I figured you could take him back for me. Just take a rope and tie him to your saddlehorn."

"Sprague's horses didn't have saddles, remember?"

"You're right. You'll figure something out."

"And balance Lena's cake on my lap at the same time," Tom said sarcastically. "Anything else while you're at it?"

"Just one more thing. Stop by the undertaker's on the way back and tell him to pick up Dillman's body. He might still be out at Lena's farm getting Brad Emmons' body. If he's not there, just leave a note. I'd do it myself, but I'm riding the other way."

"Where're you going?"

"I have an appointment," Bolt said casually. "With a schoolmarm."

"Oh?" Tom raised his eyebrows.

"Business, Tom. Strictly business. While you're enjoying the company of two pretty gals, I'll be stuck with a dowdy old schoolmarm."

Claire Jewell lived in a frame house on the edge of town. From her directions, he had no trouble finding it. He tied Nick to a hitching post out front, walked up the path and knocked on her door.

He heard the shuffle of feet and a minute later the door opened a crack. Holding a lamp in the crack of the door, Miss Jewell peeked out, then opened the door wider and invited him inside.

Bolt saw that Miss Jewell still had her glasses on, but

she had removed her hat, let her long sandy hair down. She had also changed out of her severe dress, put on a more casual house dress. With her hair down around her shoulders, she was very becoming. The glasses even added an element of mystery to her appearance.

Miss Jewell closed the door once Bolt was inside.

"Won't you come in and sit down?" she offered.

"No thanks. I'll stand." He took his Stetson hat off, held it in front of him with both hands.

"Suit yourself, but I'm glad you came."

"What was it you wanted to tell me? Something about irregularities in the ballots?"

"Yes. I saw men substitute ballot boxes for those at the polls. I think the men worked for Jack Sanders. If so, they have the legitimate boxes."

"Hell, what's the issue? Women's voting rights?"

"Not only that. I was running for office. As Mayor of Cheyenne."

"You? A woman?"

"Look, Mister Bolt," she lashed into him, "we worked hard to get women's suffrage in Wyoming. Nine years ago, Louisa Ann Swain, at the age of seventy, cast the first woman's vote. We were also allowed to hold office. No woman has done that so far. I campaigned hard and Jack Sanders wanted me to lose."

"Why? Because you're a woman?"

"No. Because my campaign platform was based on cleaning up Cheyenne, moving the bordellos out of the town limits."

Bolt was dumbfounded. He tossed his hat on a nearby chair. He looked beyond the glasses into her big brown eyes, irritated by her smug, arrogant attitude.

"Well, you sure picked the wrong man to help you out, then. I happen to own a string of whorehouses and I don't see a damned thing wrong with them. Fact is, I

154

ame to Cheyenne for the very purpose of opening up another one. So you'd better find yourself another boy. Too bad you didn't know who I was. Would have saved us both some time."

"I did know," she said. "I've heard of you."

"And you still want me to help you?"

"You're not a pimp nor a procurer. I know that much about you. From what I've heard, you give the women who work in your houses of ill repute a fair shake, treat them decently. I am not against prostitution . . ."

"You're not? But you just said . . ."

"No, I am not against prostitution. It is probably a necessary evil. But I am against it being condoned by a town, by Cheyenne."

"You're talking in riddles. Saying one thing, meaning another."

"Not really. Jack Sanders is a bad apple. I am fighting against him as much as I am against the bordellos. He's got his hands in a lot of pockets here. That's corruption, Mister Bolt, and Cheyenne will never be a decent town as long as men like Sanders have a hand in running it."

Caught up in the passion of her idealism, she took off her glasses, held them in one hand and used them to make her point.

"I agree with you there." Bolt stared into her big brown eyes, was completely mesmerized by her. He had thought of her as matronly and dowdy, but the dress she was wearing showed her figure off to advantage. She was trim, full-busted, much more petite than he had imagined. He wanted her right then and here. He didn't care what she was talking about.

"We have to get those ballot boxes back," she rattled on. "It's a matter of principle."

"If I help you, will you help me?" Bolt asked.

"If I can. If it doesn't violate my moral principles."

155

"And what are those, Miss Jewell?"

He took her in his arms, kissed her passionately. He drew her close to him, felt the warmth of her body, the large breasts pressing into his chest. He moved his hand up, squeezed one of her breasts. He was surprised when she did not back away.

She responded with a passion that she had been hiding behind her mask of being a completely proper woman.

Bolt felt her melt into his body. He felt her hand move down between his legs, grasp his growing manhood beneath the trousers.

"I want you," he husked.

"Violate my moral principles," she breathed in a low sultry voice. "Corrupt me."

CHAPTER SEVENTEEN

"Mind if I call you Claire?" Bolt asked.

"Call me anything you want," she said as she nibbled on his ear lobe.

Until now, Bolt had thought of Claire Jewell as a self-righteous snob, a woman who thought she was better than other women because she had a respectable job as a schoolmarm. But she responded to his kiss with a passion that surprised him.

He whirled her around, started unbuttoning the small buttons at the back of her dress. His nimble fingers worked them open from her neckline down past her waist. His hands slid back up to her shoulders, slipped the dress down over her arms. Her back was smooth and creamy as he ran his hands across her bare flesh.

Her dress hung up on her flared hips, gracefully draped like a mannequin's garb, without falling to the floor. She wore nothing under the dress above the waistline, but Bolt could see the slight indentation mark across her back, that told him she had been wearing a tight corset until a short while ago.

He reached around her smooth body, took a soft pliable breast in each hand. As he squeezed them, manipulated the warm flesh with his fingers, he wondered if she wore anything beneath the flowing skirt.

He turned her around to face him, kissed her again. She threw her arms around his neck as he slid his tongue inside her warm mouth. As she flicked her own playful tongue around his, he put his hands on her hips, slid her dress on down her graceful body. The garment cascaded to the rug in a heap.

Bolt's hand roamed across her bare flesh, found the furry mound between her legs. He cupped the mound, explored with his finger until he touched the fleshy lips of her sex. He ran his finger along the slit, found it warm and damp.

He felt the pressure of her hand at his crotch again, the warmth that seeped through the confining trousers. His cock throbbed, strained against the cloth of his shorts.

She backed away from the kiss, moved her lips to his ear.

"It isn't fair," she whispered with hot breath.

"What?" Bolt asked, leaning his head back to look into her pleading brown eyes.

"You've still got your clothes on," she husked as she squeezed the bulge at his crotch.

Bolt scooped her up in his arms, carried her into the bedroom, tossed her onto the bed.

"You better not just be teasing me, woman, 'cause you're gonna get it whether you want it or not."

"You threatening me, Mister Bolt?" she said, a playful tone to her voice.

"No, ma'am. Just telling you the facts." As he started to unbutton his shirt, he watched her scamper between the bed linens, pull the sheet and blanket up around her neck. He removed his gunbelt, lowered it to the floor beside the bed. The boots and socks were next. Finally he tore at the buttons of his trousers, slid them and his shorts down over his hips, pulled them off by the bottom of the pant legs.

His swollen manhood jutted out from between his legs, an arrow ready to be driven home. He saw her eyes drift down to his crotch, widen as if she were shocked by the size of his cock. He noticed that she gripped the covers a little tighter around her neck.

He stepped over to the bed, grabbed the covers and threw them back. As if by conditioned reflex, she covered her mound with one hand, tried to hide her breasts with the other.

Bolt climbed into bed next to her, leaned over to kiss her, let his hand roam across the curves of her bare flesh. He found her unresponsive to his kiss, her body rigid. He plunged his tongue between her lips, felt her lips tighten as if to keep him out. When he moved his hand down between her legs, he tried to push her hand away so that he could get close to her private parts, but she was unyielding to his gesture. She kept her hand tightly clamped across her sex.

"What gives with you, Claire?" Bolt said in an irritated tone. "I thought you wanted me and suddenly you clam up on me like some damn prick teaser!" He took his hand away from her crotch, madder than hell.

"I do want you," she said softly.

"You sure as hell have a funny way of showing it. You won't even let me touch you down there. What do you expect me to do? Stick it in your nose?"

"It's just that . . . well . . . I was almost raped a few months ago. I fought him off and when I screamed, he got scared and ran out the back door. But it left me sort of . . . sort of excited. I felt things inside me I'd never felt before. Then tonight, when I knew you were coming over, I started to fantasize what it would be like if you came here and raped me. I got so excited I even took my panties off in hopes you would just walk through the door, throw me down on the bed and take me by force. But now . . ."

"Now you've chickened out," Bolt said sarcastically.

"It's not that. It's just that the other man's . . . his . . ."

159

"Cock."

"Yes. He was drunk and his . . . organ was limp and not very big. But you're so . . . so big. I want you to rape me, but I'm afraid that you won't fit inside me."

"If you'll just relax, it'll be a perfect fit. I guarantee it." Bolt bent down to kiss her again. This time he found her lips soft and inviting.

She moved her hands up to his shoulders, spread her legs when he touched her down there. He ran his fingers across the folds of her sex, stroked the crease until he spread her legs farther apart.

He brought his hand up her body, wrapped it around one of her full breasts. He lowered his head, took one of her nipples into his mouth. As he suckled, it became a swollen nubbin in his mouth.

"Oooooh," she sighed. "That feels so good. Nobody's ever done that to me before. Take me! Take me now!"

Bolt positioned himself above her, his swollen shaft aimed at her like a heat-seeking snake. Her legs were spread wide apart to accept him. As she cooed and moaned, he reached down and splayed the lips of her sex open. He lowered his cock, touched it to the fiery flesh of her splayed lips.

Claire gasped when he touched her, started to tense up again.

"Relax," he whispered. He gave a gentle push into her oiled pussy, slid easily into her warm lips. But he could go no further. The barrier of her maidenhead was still intact. He thrust against it again, felt it weaken.

She dug her fingernails into his shoulders, tensed for his assault. "Will it hurt?" she whispered.

Before she could get the words out, Bolt plunged into her again, broke through her barrier with a quick jab.

She gasped once, then he felt her body relax, meld into his. He pumped into her with a slow, steady

160

rhythm, excited by the way her tight muscles gripped at his pulsing cock.

She became a wanton hussy beneath him, squirming and moaning like a female cat in heat. Her body bucked and undulated to match his strokes, locking him deep inside. He wanted to slow down and enjoy her for a long, long time. But each time he plunged deep inside her honeypot, it felt better than the time before. He could not pull himself away from her tight, grasping pussy long enough to settle back into nice easy strokes. Instead, he increased his thrusts, burying his cock deeper and deeper inside the folds of her sex.

He felt himself about to explode inside her and was unable to stay himself. After a couple of short strokes, he thrust his throbbing cock deep inside her and let it all happen.

After a few minutes, he rolled off of her, totally spent.

"I hope I didn't hurt you," he said.

"No," she panted, "I never knew anything could feel so good." After a long pause, she spoke again. "Bolt, do you think I'd make a good prostitute?"

"Another one of your fantasies?" Bolt smiled.

"Sort of."

"No. To be a good whore, you'd have to be ninety percent actress and have a natural hatred for men."

"But that seems contradictory. I mean, you'd have to like men to let them use your body, wouldn't you?"

"Just take my word for it, Claire. Day dreaming is a different ballgame than the hard facts of reality. There are a lot of tough old boys out there and some of them don't believe in treating a woman with respect." Bolt got up from the bed, started dressing.

"But it felt so good. I don't want this to be the only time."

"Then find yourself a nice young man who'll treat

you decent."

"But how would I find him?"

Bolt looked at her and laughed. "He'll find you. Just wear your hair down like it is now and for God's sake, don't wear that old-lady dress anymore!"

"I didn't know it was that bad," she laughed. She got up, walked to her closet, pulled out a long robe and slipped it on. "Bolt, you said you'd help me if I helped you. What did you mean by that?"

"As I told you, I came to town for the purpose of opening my own bordello here. Now that Lena Russel has lost the Lilac House, I'd like to have her manage it, risk-free, with her own girls. I'd do it outside the town limits if that's what you want, but I don't want there to be an issue about 'cleaning up Cheyenne.' I'll need the support of the ordinary townspeople, like yourself."

"Sounds fair enough to me. If we can find those real ballots, I might even be the next Mayor of Cheyenne."

Bolt fastened his gunbelt around his waist, made sure his pistol was settled in the holster. He had already reloaded the gun. He strolled into the living room where the lantern was still burning.

"So you think Sanders has the legitimate ballots and the original ballot boxes."

"I'm pretty sure of it."

"And where would he hide the ballot boxes?" Bolt wondered aloud. "I guess that's what we have to figure out next."

"I've got an idea," Claire said. "There is only one man in Cheyenne who Sanders really trusts, and that man runs the hotel where most of Sanders' men live. Sanders stays there, too, most of the time, so it's a dangerous place to go. But I think that's where they've hidden the ballot boxes."

"Where's the hotel?"

"It's a rundown place on Laramie Street called the

Arapahoe Inn."

"And who is the man who runs it?"

"Barry Jewell."

Bolt's eyebrows shot up in surprise.

"Jewell? Father? Brother?"

"Step-brother. Don't worry. There's no love lost between us. He's a drunk and a wastrel. But Sanders would use him against me if he could. Tried to, in fact, during the campaign. Barry's tough, though, and mean. So if you go there, be careful."

"Where would the boxes be kept in the hotel?"

"Barry's got a locked room in the basement. I managed to get a key to the room one day." She walked over to a desk, opened a drawer, shuffled through it and pulled out a key. She handed it to Bolt.

"You think of everything, don't you?"

"I try to. This is serious. I had hoped there would be no bloodshed, but Sanders will go to any lengths to stop me from becoming Mayor. And there's no way he wants the town cleaned up. He knows that if I could get any power at all by becoming Mayor that the townspeople just might back me up and make this a decent town again. Sanders knows he needs the protection of the sheriff and lawmen in order to survive. He also knows that that's the first thing I'd take care of. I'd fire every one of those crooked lawmen and put decent men in their places."

"Sounds like a mighty big order."

"And don't think I can't do it. But Barry is just as dangerous as Sanders. He'd do anything to stop me. He hated my mother when she married his father. And he hated me from the very beginning because he wanted to be the center of attention all the time and he thought the folks paid more attention to me than they did to him. Which was not true. Barry's father always liked him best and always wanted Barry to go places with him, like fishing and hunting, ballgames. But Barry threw a lot of tantrums and made life miserable for all of us."

"Then your name isn't Jewell," Bolt said.

"It is, because I'm adopted. I don't know who my real father is, or even if my mother was married when she had me. She never talked about it."

"How old were you when you were adopted?"

"I was seven years old when my mother married Barry's father. Barry was a year older than I was. A year later Barry's father adopted me as his own child. I think he did it to make Barry think of me as more of a sister because Barry was jealous from the start. But it just got worse after the adoption was legal. Barry was real mean to me when we were children. He pinched me and hit me and twisted my arms whenever he thought he wouldn't get caught. I used to have bruises all over my arms and legs, even cigarette burns when we got older."

"And you never told your folks?"

"No. Barry told me he'd kill me if I ever told them. And I knew he would. Barry started sneaking his father's whiskey when he was fifteen, whenever he could get away with it. When he drank that stuff, his eyes would get real wild and scary and I was afraid to be around him. Then one day . . ." She stopped short, her body shivered.

"Go ahead and talk about it," Bolt said. "It might help if you did."

She took a deep breath, started again.

"One day when I was fifteen and Barry was sixteen, the folks were going to ride into town to get supplies and they wanted me to go with them. In fact, I always went with them because I was afraid to stay home alone with Barry. But this day, Barry was gone. He'd spent the night with one of his friends and I didn't figure he'd come back until the next day. I was making a new dress for myself for the Fourth of July picnic and I told them I wanted to stay home and work on it so it would be finished in time for the picnic the next day.

"It was about a half hour after the folks left and I was sewing some lace on my dress in my bedroom when I looked up and saw Barry standing there. He was drunk, I could tell. His eyes were all wild and funny. He ripped the dress out of my hands and pushed me back on my bed. I struggled with him, but he tore my dress off of me, my panties. Then he unbuttoned his pants and pushed them down to his knees. I could see his thing and it was all red and hard. I screamed and he hit me across the face. I just kept screaming and screaming as loud as I could and he kept hitting me until I bled.

"I figured the folks would be gone about four hours, but suddenly, before Barry could put it to me, our father was standing over us. It was like a miracle. My mother had become ill and they had returned home without getting their supplies. Anyway, his father took him out to the barn and whipped him with a leather strap and then kicked him out of the house, told him he could never come back. And Barry never did live with us again. Of course, he blamed me for getting him in trouble and told me that someday he would kill me. He got in with the wrong crowd after he left home, got into all sorts of trouble. His father died a few years later of a broken heart and my mother moved away."

Claire looked drained when she had finished telling her story.

"I'm sorry," he said.

"I guess that's why I've always been afraid of sex with a man, why I always wear my hair up and wear clothes that make me look unattractive. To keep men from approaching me. And that's why I'm still afraid of

Barry. He's never forgiven me for getting him in trouble that day."

"He's a sick man, Claire. I hope you won't be afraid of other men because of him."

"You've helped a lot. Just talking to you has helped. Bolt, I'm glad you were the first one. You made it very special for me."

"I'm glad, too." He smiled. "I just hope I'm not the last."

Bolt took his hat from the chair, adjusted it on his head.

"Be careful, Bolt."

"Are you certain the ballot boxes were switched?"

"Yes. I was there when they posted the election results this morning and I didn't get any votes at all. I voted shortly after they took Lena away from the polls when she tried to vote yesterday morning. And I voted for myself! I'm sure Lena would have voted for me, and the fathers of some of the children I teach promised me their votes. So even if nobody else voted for me I would have had at least one vote."

"Well, I'll see if I can find the real ballot boxes."

"If you can, I know an honest circuit judge. Maybe we can put Jack Sanders out of business for good."

Bolt kissed Claire on the cheek, walked outside to his horse.

She made it sound so easy. Find the legitimate ballots, get Sanders convicted and sent to jail.

But he knew it wouldn't be that easy.

He was going to walk into a strange hotel that was occupied by a bunch of outlaws.

He wasn't looking forward to it at all.

CHAPTER EIGHTEEN

The key to the basement room tucked safely away in his pants pocket, Bolt rode to Laramie Street, which was several blocks away. He stopped a block away from the Arapahoe Inn, tied Nick to a hitchrail in front of a darkened market. He would go the rest of the way on foot.

He knew he was taking a chance that Barry Jewell or some of Sanders' other boys would recognize him, but it was something he had to do. Before he entered the hotel, he pulled his hat down low to hide his face. He took off his Stetson, crumpled it with his hands, rubbed it through the dirt, stomped on it a couple of times, then put it back on his head. He rumpled up his clothes, rubbed dirt on them as well. He was glad he hadn't bothered to shave that day, and that his hair was long and shaggy. He could pass as one of them.

He entered the lobby of the hotel, saw that it was even more rundown than he had thought it would be. He raised his hat briefly, keeping his arm in front of his face, while he glanced over at the reservation counter across the room. From Claire's description, he knew that Barry Jewell was the man behind the counter.

As he walked across the lobby, strangers eyed him suspiciously. He felt their hostile glares, hoped none of them recognized him.

"Yair?" barked Barry Jewell when Bolt reached the battered wood-top counter.

"Need a room for the night," Bolt said: "Downstairs. Near the back where it's quiet."

"I don't keep no quiet hours here, stranger," Barry said sarcastically. "I only got one room that ain't occupied. It's upstairs. Take it or leave it."

"I'll take it."

"Two bucks. Pay in advance."

Bolt took two dollars from his pocket, shoved it across the counter. He noticed the big hog leg single action Colt Barry had tied low on his leg.

Barry took Bolt's money, shoved the register at him. "Sign your name."

Bolt scribbled the name "Michael Stuart" on the paper, pushed it back.

"You got business here, stranger?" Barry asked suspiciously.

"Nope. Just passin' through. I'll be gone come dawn."

"Two-twelve. Room's at the front." Barry slid the key across the counter, tried to get a closer look at his face.

Bolt picked up the key, walked up the stairs and found his room. He quickly lit a lantern, closed the door. He bolted it from the inside, shoved a straight-back chair against it.

A rat darted out from under the bed, stopped to look around, then skittered across the floor, disappeared into a hole at the bottom of the wall. Bolt glanced around at the filthy room, saw the stained bed cover, the tattered curtains. The wooden floor was gouged and stained. The dresser was missing a drawer and it tilted at an angle because of a broken leg.

Even the smell in the room was foul. It smelled of sweat and urine, mildew and stale cigarette smoke. He would not turn back the covers of the bed. He knew they had not been laundered. He would not sleep anyway. He would stay in the room and wait for the chance to go down in the basement and search for the ballot boxes.

He blew out the lantern, knowing that if anyone was watching his room either from the hall or from out front, it would look like he was sleeping with the light out. He stretched out on the bed and began the long waiting. Waiting for it to become quiet downstairs. Waiting for the men to go to their rooms and go to bed.

The minutes ticked by slowly, stretched into hours. He was beginning to wonder if the noisy men would ever go to sleep or leave the hotel. After a long time, his eyelids got droopy. He fought to stay awake, kept his head and neck rigid. A couple of times, he dozed off, but awoke immediately when his head fell to the side.

When he thought he could no longer stay awake, he got up from the bed, sat on the edge. He listened carefully, heard no noise from downstairs. The hotel had finally become quiet. He walked across the floor, heard the rat scamper away. Working very quietly, he picked up the chair, moved it away from the door, eased the bolt open. He turned the door handle slowly, pulled the door open a crack. The rusty hinges creaked as he moved the door slow and easy. He moved his head and shoulders through the opening, checked to his right where there was nothing but a few more feet of wall and the end of the hall. Then he checked to his left, scanned the length of the hall. It was empty except for the litter and debris that had gathered over the past few months and never been cleaned up.

He opened the door wider, stepped out in the hall. Stepping lightly, he moved quickly down the hall to the stairway. A light from the lobby drifted up the steps, making his way easier. It could also be dangerous if anyone was watching him.

He made his way down the steps, his hand always within easy reach of his pistol. The steps groaned under his weight and he hoped the men who stayed there were so accustomed to noises in the night that they would sleep through it. He had no way of telling if Jack Sanders was staying there that night, but he knew that Barry Jewell was in one of the rooms. More than likely on the ground floor, near the registration counter.

The lobby was empty. Two flickering lanterns hung from pegs on the wall, one on each side of the lobby. He glanced up at the clock that hung on the wall behind the counter. It was after three in the morning.

There were two long halls that led off the lobby and ran to the back of the building, as far as he could tell. One of each side of the desk counter. He wished now he'd found out from Claire just exactly where the basement door was located. For all he knew, the basement door might even be outside the building. He decided to try the hallway to the right of the counter.

Just as he moved around the corner, he heard the front door swing open. He ducked down, scampered on his hands and knees around behind the counter. He heard two men talking in loud boisterous voices as they walked across the lobby. He couldn't see them but he knew they were drunk. Their speech was slurred and he could tell by their footsteps that they were staggering. They came closer, headed down the hall where he had gone. He cringed, backed down under the counter as far as he could. He saw the legs of the two men as they walked by him and on down the hall. One of the men bounced against the wall, unable to keep his balance.

A minute later, Bolt heard the sound of keys clattering against the metal locks, then one door creaked as it was opened.

"Hey, Joe," one man called, "I can't get my door open. My keysh broken."

"You're drunk, Hank," slurred the other man. "You got the wrong damn door."

The man staggered on down the hall, fumbled with

the key and lock for another few long minutes, finally opened his door and crashed inside the room. Both men must have passed out the minute they hit their beds because it was no time at all before the hotel was silent again.

In a way, Bolt was glad for the interruption. It showed him that men could come and go all hours of the night without anyone else paying any attention to them.

He scouted around for the door leading to the basement, finally found it at the end of the hall and around the corner in a little alcove off the hall. He took the key out of his pocket, tried to put it in the lock. It didn't fit. Damn. No, Claire had said there was a locked room in the basement, not that the basement door was locked.

He tried the door, saw that it was battered and loose-fitting. He'd have to force it open which would make a noise. But he had to get to the ballots. He jiggled the door, tried to break it loose without any sound. It didn't work. Finally, he leaned his shoulder into the door, gave a mighty thrust. The door opened with a resounding thud. He held his breath, waiting for someone to come running down the hall to check on the noise. He listened for footsteps, not wanting to be trapped in the basement if anyone had heard him breaking the door open.

Finally, when he didn't hear anything, he proceeded down the stairwell, cursing each step that creaked beneath him. He put the key back in his pocket, drew a match out of another pants pocket. He struck the match on his pantleg, held it up high. The small basement was a clutter of barrels and tools and boxes that were stored there. He saw the door that led to the room over in the back corner. When the match burned his fingers, he blew it out, dropped it to the ground. He felt his way across the basement, kicking his foot out in front of him as he went.

He bumped into a barrel. A box toppled off the barrel, crashed to the ground. He cursed, lit another match. He was just a few feet away from the door now. The match burned down as he reached the door. In the darkness, he felt for the keyhole, found it. He dug the key out of his pocket again, guided it into the keyhole with blind fingers. The key turned. Unlocked the door.

He opened the door, stepped just inside the room. He put the key back in his pocket for safe keeping, then took out another match and struck it into flame. He saw them then. There, in a corner, were the legitimate ballot boxes. The Telegraph Matches crates that had been converted into ballot boxes by chiseling slots for the ballots in the lid.

He heard a sound behind him. He froze for an instant, then dropped the match, drew his pistol with the speed of lightning. He whirled around, could not see anything in the darkness.

Then, something crashed into the top of his head. Pain shot through to his brain.

He pitched forward into the darkness. He fell to the floor, unconscious.

Lena Russel couldn't stand it anymore. It was three-thirty in the morning according to the clock on the wall of the expensive hotel room. She was worried about Bolt. Tom had told her, during dinner, that Bolt had an appointment and that he would probably be back in about two hours. She had thought he would be back by nine or ten o'clock, but now that it was so late, she wondered if he had run into trouble.

She wondered who he had an appointment with. She knew that she had no holds on Bolt, that he was free to go where he wanted, but she was terribly worried that something had happened to him.

Finally, she knew she had to go next door and talk to Tom, no matter what the hour. She hated to wake Tom and Carmen up, but she couldn't wait until morning. Not with Bolt's life at stake. She slipped a robe over her nightgown, walked down the hall to the next room. She tapped lightly on the door.

"Who is it?" said Tom's sleepy voice a minute later.

"Lena," she said in a loud whisper.

Tom opened the door and let her in. He had slipped into his trousers, lit a lantern before he opened the door. He yawned, ran his fingers through his tousled hair. Carmen raised her head, looked at Lena from the bed across the room. When she saw who it was, she grabbed her duster robe from a nearby chair, put it over her gown and got up.

"What's the matter?" Carmen asked.

"Hell, what time is it?" Tom yawned.

"It's Bolt," said Lena. "He isn't back yet and it's almost four in the morning."

"I thought he was back long ago," Tom said. "He said he'd only be a couple of hours. Wonder where he is." Tom was worried now, too.

"Do you know where he went?" Lena asked.

"No. He didn't tell me. Just said something about a schoolmarm."

Lena thought for a minute. "He must have met Claire Jewell. Yes. It would have to be her. Oh, Tom, will you take me there?"

"Can't it wait till morning?" Tom said.

"It is morning! Claire might know something!"

Yes, Tom thought, and Bolt also might be spending the night with the schoolmarm. Could be embarrassing if he took Lena there.

"Tom, Bolt's in trouble. I just know he is! If you don't want to go to Claire's with me, I'll have to go myself."

"No, I'll go with you. I'm worried about him myself. Do you know where she lives?"

"Yes. She's a friend of mine."

"Is it close enough to walk?"

"We could, but it's clear across town."

"I'll borrow Sprague's horses again. Go put some warm clothes on. It's cold out there."

"Do you want me to go with you?" Carmen offered.

"No, you stay here," Tom said. "Keep the bed warm."

Lena was dressed in a heavy dress and a coat by the time Tom was ready to go. Outside, a lantern hung on the wall by the back door. It made it easier for Tom to round up the horses from the fenced yard. They rode bareback across town, knocked on Claire's door and woke her up. When she let them in, Lena asked her if Bolt had been there.

Claire told them about the switched ballot boxes and said that Bolt had gone to get the legitimate boxes from the Arapahoe Hotel.

"It's a very dangerous place," she said, "because so many of Sanders' men live there."

"Can we get the sheriff to go there?" Tom asked.

"Some of the deputies are on Sanders' payroll. It would be useless to try."

"Well, I've got to go there and find out what happened to Bolt. It shouldn't have taken him this long. You girls stay here until I get back."

"No," they both said at once.

"I'm going with you," said Lena.

"I'll go too," said Claire. "I'm a pretty fair shot and you just might need some help."

CHAPTER NINETEEN

Bolt woke up, didn't know where he was. The room was brightly lit. He started to raise his head. Pain shot through the top of his head. Then he remembered. Someone had hit him on top of the head. In the basement.

Suddenly, he realized that he was tied to a bed. Spread-eagle, with his hands tied to the head of the bed, his feet lashed to the brass bedposts at the foot of the bed. He struggled to free his hands from their tight bindings, but the thongs only became tighter around his wrists as he fought them. He kicked with his feet, but could not free those bindings either. He didn't know who had hit him or where he was, but he knew he had to get out of there.

He glanced around him, looking for something that he could use to help free himself. When he saw the shabby furniture, the stained and tattered curtains, he realized that he was in a room just like the one he'd been in earlier. It wasn't the same room, but he knew he was still at the Arapahoe Hotel.

He grunted and groaned, tried to get at least one hand free.

In the next room, a young woman heard him moan. She got up from her chair, walked into the room where Bolt was tied down. She was following Barry Jewell's orders.

Bolt looked up when she entered the room. He was surprised to see the young woman. He raised his head despite the pain, saw that she was a pretty, dark-

175

skinned girl with black hair, dark eyes, and the look of an Indian.

"Who are you?" he asked.

"My name is Hawk Lady," she said. "Barry Jewell has asked me to guard you. Now that you are awake, I will stay with you until he returns."

"Is he the one who conked me on the head?"

"Yes. He told me that. He said you were in the basement where you didn't belong."

"Does Barry know who I am? What my name is?"

"He said your name was Michael Stuart, that you had checked into the hotel late last night. Barry has gone to bring Sanders here so they can decide what should be done with you for snooping around in the basement."

"Will you untie me, Hawk Lady?"

"No. I cannot do that. I am Barry's woman. I do what he tells me to do. I am only to guard you."

As she stood over him, he saw the blueblack bruise on her cheek, the circle around her eye that was darker than her skin, the scar above her eye.

"Did Barry beat you?" he asked.

"Yes, that is his way."

"You don't have to put up with that," Bolt said, enraged by what he saw. "Barry has no right to hit you."

"But I am his woman."

"That's why I'm here. Why I was in the basement. I'm here because Claire Jewell is fighting to make this a better town. She is fighting for the rights of all women, so they won't get beat up like you have been."

"I know Claire. I like her. I feel sorry for her."

"Don't you see why you have to untie me? You can free yourself at the same time."

"But you cannot beat these men. They are very strong."

"You can beat them," he told her. "I can, if you'll give me the chance."

"I don't know. Barry would not like it if I let you go. Who are you anyway?"

"The name is Bolt."

"I have heard of you and what you have done. I know of the hatred Barry carries for his half-sister. It is a violent hatred which goes back to childhood. He talks of it when he is drunk and at those times I fear for her life. He thinks his father loved her best and he has carried his resentment all these many years. He gets crazy when he drinks and talks about the hatred. It scares me."

"Do you love Barry, Hawk Lady?"

She hung her head, lowered her eyes. "No, I do not love Barry. He does not love me either. I am little more than a slave to him. He beats me and uses my body for his own pleasures. But it is quick when we are in bed together and I do not mind so much. It is better than the beatings. I bring him whiskey so he can get drunk and rave."

"Can't you leave him, get away from him?"

"I seldom go anywhere, but I must always return to him. He bought me from the Blackfeet, so I must do what he says. I am his woman."

"No, you're wrong. You're your own woman. You don't have to live this way. He doesn't own your life. If you will untie me, I will see to it that you have your own life, free of Barry forever."

"I can see that you would be a gentle lover," she said boldly. "Barry will not like it, but I will free you on one condition. I would like to get away from him, yes, but first I want you to make love to me. I want you to show me what it is like with a real man."

"Well, I don't know," Bolt said. That's all he needed now. To be making love to Barry's woman when Barry came back. But he had to get free of the bindings.

"Please, Bolt." Her dark eyes pleaded with him.

"What about Barry? Is there time?"

"Yes. There is time. Barry was very drunk when he left here and he did not want Sanders to see him that way. He did not want to wake him up so early either. Barry will go to a bathhouse and sober up before he tells Sanders about you. There is time."

She cut the thongs on his feet first, using a sharp knife from the dresser. Then she cut through the ties of his wrists.

He rubbed his wrists, watched her strip out of her dark dress, her undergarments. As she took off her clothes, he saw the other bruises that covered her body.

When she was naked, she stepped over to the bed and unbuttoned Bolt's shirt, took it off, then removed his trousers. Bolt realized that his gunbelt was gone, his pistol.

She got in the bed with him, took his soft mass of flesh in her hand and began kneading it with delicate fingers. It began to grow in her hand. When it was hard, she lowered her head, took it inside her mouth. She suckled it, flicked her tongue across the tip end. She took it deep in her mouth, then bobbed back and forth along its swollen length, sucking hard as she did.

"That feels good," he said.

"This is what I must do with Barry. It is the only way he can get hard enough to enter me. I don't like to do it to him, but with you it is different. I like the way you feel in my mouth. I like your smell. You make me very excited."

"Do you want me inside you now?"

"Yes, please."

Bolt was very gentle with the Hawk Lady when he took her. She had suffered enough and he would not

178

hurt her now. She was passionate like she'd never known passion before and Bolt could tell that it was the first time she had ever enjoyed the act. He knew, by her actions, that it was the first time she had responded with her own emotions instead of merely tolerating the actions of Barry.

Bolt felt her tremble with an orgasm and knew that it, too, was a first for her.

He wanted to make love to her for a long time, but he knew they had to hurry. He knew he had made her feel good and maybe that was enough for now. He pumped into her with his swollen cock, sank deep into her dark folds. He found her strangely exciting the way she rocked beneath him and he exploded his seed deep inside her even as he wanted her more.

Sanders had spent the night in his little hide-out shack, a short two blocks from the Arapahoe Hotel. Barry was the only one who knew where he was so he felt safe there.

It was almost daylight when Barry knocked on his door. Sanders woke with a start, heard Barry calling his name. He had slept in his clothes like he usually did, too drunk to know the difference. He opened the door and let Barry in.

"What in the hell are you doing here at this time of the night?" Sanders yelled.

"It's morning, almost," Barry said. "I found a man poking around in the basement during the middle of the night. I think he was looking for the ballot boxes. At least that's where I found him. I thought you'd want to know."

"Anyone we know?"

"A man called Michael Stuart. He checked into the hotel last night. But don't worry. I knocked him out cold. He's still out. He's tied to the bed."

"What'd he look like?" Sanders asked, his suspicions aroused.

"Dark shaggy hair, a beat-up Stetson, about six foot tall. I didn't get a good look at his face when he checked in 'cause he kept his hat brim pulled down over his face. But I saw him after I knocked him out. Kinda ordinary looking."

"That was Bolt, you asshole. I've been looking all over town for that bastard! He shows up at the hotel and nobody recognizes him!"

"He kept his face hidden. I told you that."

"That should have given you a clue right there. Who's watching him now?"

"Hawk Lady."

"That fucking halfbreed? You stupid bastard! Come on, let's get over there before the whimpering bastard convinces her to let him go."

"Hawk Lady wouldn't do that! She's my woman. She does what I tell her to do."

"Thank you, Bolt," said Hawk Lady. "You have made me a real woman. I will be free for the rest of my life."

"Not if Barry comes back and finds you here. You'd better leave now."

"No, I want to stay and help you. I owe you that much."

"You don't owe me anything. I have to go back down to the basement and get those ballot boxes. That's the only way we can prove that the election was crooked. It's the only way we can get Barry and Sanders sent to prison. Without those boxes, the women of Cheyenne will lose their right to vote, including you."

"You mean I will be able to vote?"

"How old are you?"

"Eighteen."

"You'll be able to vote, all right, but you'll have to wait three years. But if we don't hurry, neither one of us will have a chance to vote. Barry could be back here with Sanders anytime."

Bolt got into his clothes as fast as he could.

Hawk Lady walked over to the dresser, opened a drawer and lifted out Bolt's gunbelt and pistol, handed it to him. "You'll need this."

"Thank you. You're a good woman, Hawk Lady."

Hawk Lady put on her dress and panties, the moccasins she always wore.

When Bolt opened the door and stepped out into the hall, he realized that he had been in the room next to the one he had taken for the night. On the second floor. Together, they ran down the flight of stairs, across the lobby. Just as they turned down the hallway that led to the basement door, they heard someone walk into the lobby from the other hallway. Bolt froze in his tracks. Hawk Lady stopped, put her finger to her lips, a gesture for silence. She eased back along the wall, peeked around the corner into the lobby, then moved on quiet moccasins back to Bolt. She pulled him on down the hall, waited until they were at the back to speak.

"It's just the desk clerk," she whispered. "He works the morning shift and he always comes in early. Don't worry about him. He's used to people wandering around at all hours and besides, he's not very bright."

"Did he see you?"

"No. He was looking the other way."

Bolt opened the door to the basement and the two of them went down the stairs. He was so close to getting his hands on the ballot boxes that would put Sanders away for a long time. He hoped he wasn't too late.

*   *   *

Tom and the two women, Lena and Claire, rode as fast as they could toward the Arapahoe Hotel. When they were a block away, Tom spotted Bolt's horse tied to the hitching post.

"Looks like he's still there," he said.

"How can you tell from here?" Claire asked.

"That's his horse. If he had left the hotel, he would have taken Nick with him."

"Oh, no, something's happened to him," cried Lena. "I just know it."

"Let's hope not," Tom said. His guts churned when he thought about it. He knew the chances of finding Bolt alive were slim, especially after what Claire had said about all of Sanders' men staying at the hotel. He couldn't stand to think of losing Bolt after all these years. They had been through a hell of a lot together, were closer than brothers. And Bolt had been in some mighty tight spots before, but nothing as dangerous as now.

"I can't think that way," Lena said. "Bolt told me that I should think positive thoughts. He said to always have faith in the things I wanted and that that would make them come true. Well, I want him to be alive, so I will keep my faith that he is."

"Good advice for all of us," Tom said. "I think we'd better tie our horses here with Bolt's and walk the rest of the way."

The girls agreed. After they tied the horses up, they walked to the Arapahoe Hotel. The sky was beginning to lighten in the east. It would be daylight soon.

"You girls wait outside," Tom said firmly. "I don't know what I'll be walking into and I don't want you to go in there until I know what we're up against."

Claire started to challenge him, but changed her mind. Tom was right. It would be easier for him to go in and find Bolt than all three of them trapsing through the hotel.

"We'll go across the street to the restaurant and have a cup of coffee," she said. "But, Tom, please let us know as soon as you find out anything."

"I will."

"Be careful," Lena said. She was on the verge of tears, but she tried to be light hearted. "Tell Bolt that I'll buy him breakfast."

"What about me?" Tom laughed, although he, too, was scared.

"Hell, I'll buy everybody breakfast. Just bring him out alive."

CHAPTER TWENTY

Tom walked into the lobby of the hotel. He had hoped there would be no one there so he could search for Bolt, but the desk clerk spotted him the minute he walked through the door.

"Can I help you, sir?" the clerk called.

Tom strolled over to the counter, spoke in a low voice.

"I'm looking for a friend of mine. Thought he might be here. Mind if I look around?"

"Oh, I couldn't let you do that. If you'll tell me his name, I can tell you whether he's staying with us or not."

"The name's Bolt."

"Never heard the name before. When did he check in?"

"Last night, probably." Tom figured he was wasting valuable time. He didn't think Bolt would have registered. Unless he had used the room to get inside the building.

"I wasn't here last night," said the clerk. He checked the register. "Nope. Nobody by that name here. Last name checked in is Michael Stuart."

"Might be him," said Tom. "His brother's name is Michael and sometimes he uses that name. What's the room number?"

"Two-twelve. But don't you think it's a bit early to go calling?"

"Oh, that's O.K. He's an early riser."

Tom walked up the stairs, found room 212. He tried

the door, found it open. The early morning light filtered through the tattered curtains and Tom could see that the room was empty. He looked around to see if he could find any clues that Bolt had been there. The bed hadn't been slept in, but the covers were wrinkled as if someone had lain down for a while. Claire had said the ballot boxes were in the basement. He'd have to try there, see if he could find his friend.

He was just ready to step out into the hall when he heard voices. He tucked back into the room, leaned against the wall.

The door to the next room opened.

"He's gone!" cried Barry Jewell. "They're both gone."

"I told you that fucking halfbreed was no damned good," Sanders bellowed.

"Maybe they're next door. In Bolt's room."

Tom held his breath, looked around for a hiding place.

"What the hell would they go there for, you idiot?" Sanders said. "Downstairs. To the basement. Quick!"

Tom heard the two men run back down the hall, down the flight of stairs. He stepped out into the hall, followed them at a distance so he wouldn't be seen.

The two men dashed across the lobby, down the hall to the door that led to the basement.

Bolt carried the two ballot boxes in his arms. Hawk Lady was right behind him on the stairwell that went from the basement to the ground floor. They were halfway up the stairs when they heard Sanders' voice. They tried to back down, but were spotted.

"There he is!" yelled Barry.

Sanders fired a quick shot down the stairwell.

Bolt saw what was happening before Sanders got the shot off. He shoved Hawk Lady out of the way. Sanders' shot had been too quick. Too high.

Bolt whipped out his pistol, returned Sanders' fire. But Sanders had ducked away from the opening, hid behind the wall until he could get another shot off. Bullets flew as Barry drew and fired.

Bolt backed down the stairs, kept going until he backed into the small storeroom. Hawk Lady was right behind him. He knew he was trapped with no other way out but the stairs. If the gunfire brought more of Sanders' men, he wouldn't have a chance.

Sanders and Barry stood at the top of the stairs, peered into the darkness below them. They could no longer see Bolt, didn't know where he was. They were afraid to go down the stairs for fear of getting shot.

Tom snuck up behind the two men.

"Drop your weapons!" he ordered.

It was a mistake.

Sanders snarled, whirled around and fired at Tom. The bullet caught Tom in the arm. His pistol dropped from his hand, clattered down the stairs.

Tom clutched his arm, pressed the wound to stop the bleeding. He heard a sound behind him, turned around. When he saw who it was, he moved away from the opening.

Bolt heard Tom's voice, heard the shot. He stepped out of the room to see what had happened.

Sanders saw Bolt again. At the bottom of the stairwell where the light shone down. He hammered back for the killing shot.

"Here I come, Sanders," Bolt yelled, charging up two of the steps.

Hawk Lady ran out of the storeroom, tried to stop Bolt from running up the stairs.

Barry saw her. He drew a bead on her, held it as a cruel smile crossed his lips.

In the confusion, Sanders lost his aim on Bolt. He steadied his pistol, aimed again.

For a moment, Hawk Lady stared up at Barry, her eyes wide.

"I'll kill you, bitch!" Barry spat.

"No you won't!" came a shrill high-pitched woman's voice from behind Barry and Sanders.

Sanders turned to see who it was, then swung back on Bolt. Bolt was quicker. He fired before Sanders could get his shot off. The bullet smashed into Sanders' head. His arms flew up in the air. He collapsed, tumbled halfway down the stairs, dead at Bolt's feet.

Barry ran part way down the stairs to get a better shot at Hawk Lady. He glanced back up to see who had called out to him.

At the top of the stairs, Claire Jewell stood with her feet apart. In her hand was a pistol. It was already cocked and aimed at Barry.

Barry hesitated when he saw his step-sister. He wanted to shoot both women. He decided against Hawk Lady for the moment as his hatred for Claire boiled over. He bared his teeth, swung his gun arm around to shoot Claire in the heart.

She dropped him with a shot to the chest.

Barry staggered backwards, clawed at the wall to pull himself back up the stairs. He couldn't believe his step-sister had shot him. He had to kill her. He made it to the top, toppled over on the floor, his head at her feet.

"I—I hate you," he babbled.

"No, Barry," she said quietly. "You hate yourself. You always did. You made the trouble in the family. Your father always loved you the best, but you couldn't see it. I feel only pity for you. I'm sorry."

Barry tried to say something, but his eyes glazed over in death before he could get the words out. Claire hoped he understood before he died that he had been loved.

Bolt went back down and got the ballot boxes. He carried them up the stairs, stepped over Sanders' body. Hawk Lady was right beside him. She picked up Tom's gun from the stairs, held it in her hands.

"Let's go out in the lobby where there's some light," Bolt said. "I want to look at that arm of yours, Tom."

Claire and Hawk Lady followed the two men as they walked along the hall to the brightly lit lobby. The morning light was just beginning to come through the windows out front.

Bolt looked at Tom's arm. He saw that the bullet had grazed the flesh but it hadn't penetrated it. The bleeding had already stopped.

"You got a nasty gash there," Bolt told his friend, "but you'll probably pull through."

"You mean I got to look at your ugly face for a few more years?"

"Could be worse."

Hawk Lady handed Tom his pistol. He thanked her, then turned to Claire.

"I thought I told you not to come in here. But I'm glad you did."

"Well, here are the ballot boxes," Bolt told Claire. "Looks like you won."

"Maybe I didn't. But at least we'll get a fair count."

"Have we still got a deal?"

"Either way, Bolt, you've got a deal. If Lena goes for it, that is."

"I think I can answer that," Tom said. "She'll go for anything you have in mind. The woman's been up all night worrying about you."

A twinge of jealousy passed through Claire's thoughts, but she knew she was bigger than that. Bolt had taught her a lot and now she wasn't afraid to go out and find her own man.

"By the way," Bolt said. "Where's Lena? Still back at

the hotel?"

"No, she's at the restaurant across the street," said Tom. "Waiting to buy you breakfast."

Claire walked over to Hawk Lady, smiled at the sad halfbreed. "Come on, Hawk Lady. My home is big enough for a couple of spinsters."

"Claire," said Bolt, "if you'll take those glasses off once in a while and let your hair down you won't be a spinster for long."

She laughed, took off her glasses.

Tom whistled.

Bolt kissed the two women on the cheeks, gave them each a hug.

"Claire, is there room at your home for Bolt, too?" Hawk Lady asked. "He is much man. More than enough to go around."

"Yes, I think I know what you mean," smiled Claire. "Too much man for any one woman."

"Looks like you got all the charm, Bolt," said Tom. "And before it gets any thicker in here, I'm going to escort these two lovely ladies to the horses. Claire has her own horse and I'll let Hawk Lady take one of Sprague's horses, if you don't mind riding double on your horse, Bolt."

"With you?"

"No. With Lena."

"You had me worried there for a minute."

"And if it's all right with you ladies," Tom said, "I'll come by later this afternoon to get Sprague's horse."

"Are you much man like Bolt?" Hawk Lady giggled.

"More man!"

"You're full of bullshit, Tom. I'm going to go see Lena."

"I'll be there shortly. Order me double of whatever you get."

Bolt walked out the door and across the street.

He saw Lena through the restaurant window. She looked so sad and lonely.

He went inside, walked up behind her before she spotted him.

"I came to take you up on your breakfast invitation," Bolt said.

Lena jumped a foot. When she realized it was Bolt, she stood up and threw her arms around him.

"Oh, thank God you're all right."

"Did you ever have any doubts?"

"No never."

"You're going to get a brand new bordello. I'm going to buy it for you and I want you to run it with your girls. It'll be outside of the town limits, but let the town come to you."

"Oh, Bolt, that's wonderful!"

"What are you going to name it? Lilac House Number Two?"

"No. I like the color, but the name leaves a bad taste in my mouth now. Let's see, I think I'll call it The Purple Palace. Do you like that?"

"I've got a better name. And it fits you."

"What's that?"

"The Purple Passion Palace."

He ducked as she picked up a cloth napkin and threw it at him.

MORE FANTASTIC READING FROM ZEBRA!

THE SURVIVALIST SERIES
by Jerry Ahern